T Collins

Easy Translations from Latin Prose

T Collins

Easy Translations from Latin Prose

ISBN/EAN: 9783337371005

Printed in Europe, USA, Canada, Australia, Japan

Cover: Foto ©Andreas Hilbeck / pixelio.de

More available books at **www.hansebooks.com**

EASY TRANSLATIONS

FROM

LATIN PROSE AUTHORS

FOR

RETRANSLATION INTO LATIN.

WITH NOTES.

BY

T. COLLINS, M.A.,

HEAD MASTER OF THE LATIN SCHOOL, NEWPORT, SALOP.

LONDON:

GEORGE BELL AND SONS, YORK STREET,

COVENT GARDEN.

1888.

PREFACE.

For some time past, not knowing a book sufficiently easy for the purpose, I have been in the habit of translating easy passages of Cæsar, Nepos, &c., for retranslation into Latin prose. Thinking that some of my brother masters may have experienced a similar difficulty and be glad of a book of the sort, I have ventured to publish one. With each piece is given the author, &c., from which it comes, so that any master will be able to refer to the passage. I may add that the passages are intended to be done in school without a dictionary, and to be of the standard of the Oxford and Cambridge Local Examinations.

T. Collins.

EASY PASSAGES FOR RETRANSLATION.

I. *NEPOS.*

When the news of Xerxes' approach reached Greece, and the Athenians especially were said to be[1] his object in consequence of the battle of Marathon,[2] they sent to Delphi to ask[3] what[4] they should do concerning their affairs. The priestess replied that they should protect themselves with their wooden walls. When no one knew the meaning[5] of that reply, Themistocles persuaded them that it was the advice of Apollo that they should put[6] themselves and their property on board[6] ship. Having[7] approved of such a plan, they add to their former ships as many[8] again, and carry off all their property that could be moved, partly to Salamis and partly to Trœzen. They hand over the Acropolis[9] and the performance[10] of sacred rites to the priests and a few elderly men, and leave the rest of the town.—*Themistocles*, 2.

[1] *Peti.*

[2] Use an adjective. Cf. *pugna Cannensis*, the battle of Cannæ.

[3] You cannot use infinitive of the purpose. You may use *ut* or *qui* with subj., the supine in *um*, *causâ* with genitive of gerund, or future participle.

[4] In a dependent sentence the verb is in the subjunctive.

[5] The Latins are fond of dependent sentences, so say "what that reply meant."

[6] *Se conferre in naves.*

[7] Abl. abs.   [8] *Totidem.*   [9] *Arx.*

[10] *Sacra procuranda.* The latter is a technical word.

II. *CÆSAR.*

To carry[1] out these arrangements Orgetorix is chosen. He undertook[2] an embassy to the states. On that journey he persuades[3] Casticus, the son of Catamanta- ledes, whose father had possessed[4] sovereign[5] power among the Sequani for many years, and had been called friend by the Senate of the Roman people, to seize[6] upon the sovereignty in his state, which his father had pre- viously held, and he also persuades Dumnorix, an Æduan, the brother of Divitiacus, who at that time held the chief position in the state, and was especially in favour[7] with the common people, to make the same attempt, and he gives[8] him his daughter in marriage.—*Bell. Gall.* i. 3.

[1] Use the gerundive of *conficio* with *ad.*

[2] *Suscipere sibi.*

[3] *Persuadeo* takes the dative and *ut* with subjunctive.

[4] *Obtineo.* Do not translate it by "obtain." Cf. *familia, officium, religio,* etc., which do not mean the English words derived from them.

[5] *Regnum.*

[6] *Occupare.*

[7] *Acceptus plebi.*

[8] The Latins say *dare in matrimonium.*

III. *CÆSAR.*

When the Helvetii were informed[1] of his approach, they send as ambassadors to him the most noble men of the state, to say[2] that they intended[3] to march through the province without (doing) any harm,[4] because[5] they had no other route; that they asked that it might be allowed them to do this with his consent.[6] Cæsar, because he recollected that Cassius the consul had been slain and his army sent under the yoke, did not think that it ought to be granted[7]; nor did he think that men hostilely[3] disposed, when an opportunity was allowed them of marching through the province, would abstain from injury and outrage. Nevertheless, that time might intervene until the soldiers assembled, he answered the ambassadors, "I[9] will take a day to deliberate; if you wish anything, return on the 12th of April."—*Bell. Gall.* i. 7.

[1] *Certiorem aliquem facere de aliquo.*

[2] Use *qui* with subjunctive.

[3] Cf. *mihi est in animo.*

[4] *Maleficium.*

[5] *Quod* denotes here what they said, and must therefore have subj.

[6] *Voluntas.*

[7] *Concedo.* Lit. "that it was not to be granted."

[3] *Inimico animo*, abl. of quality.

[9] Put to end into oratio obliqua, and recollect that the imperative in Direct goes into the pres. or imperfect subjunctive in Oblique Narration.

IV. *NEPOS*.

Now[1] Hamilcar, as soon as he had crossed the sea and come to Spain, performed with success[2] great achievements; subdued very great and warlike nations; enriched[3] the whole of Africa with horses, men, and money. He was killed fighting in battle against the Vettones in the ninth year after he had come into Spain, when he was thinking[4] of making[5] war on Italy. His undying[6] hatred towards the Romans appears to have principally caused[7] the second Punic war. For Hannibal his son was induced[8] by the constant adjurations[9] of his father to prefer to perish rather than not measure[10] himself with the Romans.—*Hamilcar*, 4.

[1] Not by *nunc*, except when it refers to time. *At* or *autem* (never first word) will do.

[2] *Secunda fortuna.* Cf. *res secundæ, secundo flumine.*

[3] *Locupleto.*

[4] *Meditor.*

[5] *Inferre bellum in.*

[6] *Perpetuus.*

[7] *Concito.*

[8] *Eo perductus est ut.*

[9] *Obtestatio.*

[10] *Experior.*

V. *CICERO.*

Themistocles, after his victory in that war which was with the Persians, said at a public meeting, that he had a plan beneficial for the state, but that it was necessary that it should not be known. He demanded that the people should appoint some one to whom he might im-part[1] it. Aristides was appointed. He told him that the fleet of the Lacedæmonians which had been beached at Gytheum could be secretly burnt ; that when this was done, the power of the Lacedæmonians must be crushed. When Aristides had heard this, he came to the assembly mid[3] great excitement, and said that the plan was a very useful one which Themistocles proposed,[4] but that it was very dishonourable.—*De Off.* iii. 11.

[1] *Concio.*
[2] The Latins say *communicare cum aliquo.*
[3] *Subducere navem* is to draw a ship up on the beach. The opposite expression is *deducere navem.*
[4] *Opes.*
[5] *Magnâ expectatione.*
[6] *Affero.*

VI. *SALLUST.*

Marius arrived [1] at Zama.   This town, situated in a
plain, was fortified rather by engineering [2] than by nature,
lacking [3] nothing necessary, rich in arms and men.
Therefore Metellus, having prepared matters as [4] the
occasion and ground required, surrounds all the walls
with his army, and orders his staff-officers [5] where each
one should direct [6] operations.   Then, on a signal being
given, a mighty shout arises from all sides at once, nor
does that terrify the Numidians; with hostile [7] front and
eager [8] for the fray they remain without confusion; the
battle is commenced.   Some of the Romans fought [9] at
a distance with bullets [10] or stones, others approached
and at one time [14] undermined [11] the wall, at another [14] as-
sailed [12] it with ladders,[13] desiring to fight hand to hand.
—*Jugurtha,* 57.

[1] *Pervenire ad.*
[2] *Opere* or *manu.*
[3] *Egeo.*   Cf. *Mancipiis locuples eget æris Cappadocum rex.*
[4] *Pro tempore atque loco.*
[5] *Legati.*
[6] *Curo.*   When followed by a verb, the verb is put in the gerundive.
Cf. *Curabo pontem faciendum.*
[7] *Infensi.*
[8] *Intenti.*
[9] Cf. *eminus* (*e manu*) and *comminus* (*con manus*) *pugnare.*
[10] *Glans,* literally an acorn.
[11] *Subfodio.*   The word for a mine is *cuniculus.*
[12] *Aggredior.*
[13] *Scala.*
[14] *Modo—modo* or *nunc—nunc.*

VII. *CICERO.*

Ariobarzanes, a king, the ally and friend of the Roman people, has been banished from his kingdom ; two kings menace [1] all Asia, most hostile [2] not only to you, but also to your allies and friends ; all states, moreover,[3] the whole of Asia and Greece, are compelled by the magnitude of the danger, to look [4] for your aid.   They neither dare to demand a particular [5] commander from you, especially since you have sent them another, nor do they think that they can do so without the greatest danger.   They see and feel the same [6] that you do, that there is one man in whom all things are in perfection,[7] and that he is at hand, by whose mere [8] arrival and name, although he came to the maritime war, they yet perceive the raids [9] of the enemy were checked [10] and retarded.—*De lege Pio. Manilia,* 5.

[1] *Immineo,* followed by dative.

[2] *Inimicus.*

[3] *Autem.*   This word cannot stand first ; so also *quoque, quidem, que,* etc.

[4] *Expectare.*

[5] *Certus.*

[6] *Idem—quod.*

[7] *Summus.*   This is the superlative of *superus,* contracted for *supremus.*

[8] *Ipse.*

[9] *Impetus* or *incursiones.*

[10] *Reprimo.*

VIII. *CICERO.*

He meets[1] Clodius in front of his farm about five[2] in the evening, or thereabouts.[3]   Immediately several men with weapons attack[4] him from the higher ground ; those in front slay the charioteer.[5]   But when Milo, throwing aside his great coat,[6] had sprung[7] from his carriage and was defending himself with great spirit, some of those who were with Clodius, having[8] drawn their swords, began[9] to run back to the carriage to attack Milo in[10] the rear, while others, because they thought that he was by this time killed, begin to cut down his slaves who were behind.—*Pro Milone,* 10.

[1] *Obviam ire* or *fieri alicui.*

[2] The Latins divided the day into twelve hours, beginning at six in the morning, and the night into four watches of three hours each, beginning at six in the evening.   Thus five o'clock will be the eleventh hour.

[3] *Non multo secus.*

[4] *Impetum facere in aliquem.*

[5] *Rhedarius.*

[6] *Pænula.*

[7] *Desilio.*

[8] Abl. abs.

[9] Use historical infinitives.

[10] *A tergo.*   Similarly *a fronte, a latere.*

IX. *CÆSAR.*

Now [1] when our men hesitated,[2] principally because of the depth of the sea, he who bore the eagle of the tenth legion, having appealed [3] to heaven that this might turn out prosperously for the legion, says " Leap [4] down, my fellow soldiers,[5] unless you wish to betray the eagle to the enemy ; I, at any rate, shall [6] have performed my duty to the state and my commander." Having [7] said this in a loud voice, he threw himself from the ship and began to carry the eagle against the foe. Then our men, exhorting one [8] another, leapt down in a body [9] from the ship.—*Bell. Gall.* iv. 25.

[1] Abl. abs.	[6] Fut. perfect of *præsto.*
[2] *Cunctor.*	[7] *Quum* with pluperfect subj.
[3] *Deos contestatus.*	[8] *Inter se.*
[4] *Desilio.*	[9] *Universi.*
[5] *Commilito.*	

X. *CÆSAR.*

This state is by far the most powerful of the whole [1] of Gaul in cavalry, and has great forces of infantry, and borders [2] on the Rhine, as we have mentioned above. In this state two men were striving together for the chief-power. [3] The one [4] of these, as soon as he heard [5] of the arrival of Cæsar and the legions, came to him. He assured him that he and his men would remain [6] loyal, and would not revolt from the friendship of the Roman [7] people. But the other, Indutiomarus, began to collect cavalry and infantry, and having hidden [8] in the woods those who, owing to their age, were unable to bear arms, to prepare for war.—*Bell. Gall.* v. 3.

---

[1] *Totus, reliquus, medius, summus,* etc., agree with the substantive, e.g. *tota Gallia, summus mons.*

[2] *Tango.*

[3] *Principatus.*

[4] *Alter.*

[5] Use verb impersonally.

[6] *Esse in officio.*

[7] *Romanus populus,* never *Romani populi. Populi* means nations.

[8] *Abdo in* (with the accusative).

[XI. *LIVY.*]

They fought for about three hours, and everywhere fiercely. The battle, however, round the Consul was more fierce and deadly.[2] He was followed by the flower of the soldiers, and he himself, wherever he perceived his men were hard pressed and in difficulties,[4] vigorously took them assistance. At length an Insubrian knight, recognizing the Consul by his appearance, said to his countrymen, "Lo, this is he who has laid[6] low our legions and has laid[7] waste our country and our city! Now I will offer this victim to the shades[8] of my countrymen foully slain," and having applied[9] spurs to his horse, he charged[10] through the thickest[11] ranks of the enemy, and having first cut down the armour-bearer, who had opposed his hostile advance, he pierced the Consul with his spear. The veterans[12] with shields opposed kept him off when he desired to spoil him.—(xxii. 6.)

---

[1] Use the verb impersonally.

[2] *Infestus. Infensus* is used of the feelings, cf. *quid nisi mens infensa infestam torqueat hastam?*

[3] The English passive may often be translated by the Latin active, and conversely, e.g. *pavor cepit milites*, the soldiers were seized with panic.

[4] *Robur.*   [5] *Laborare.*   [6] *Cado.*   [7] *Depopulor.*

[8] *Manes*, only used in the plural.

[9] *Subdere calcaria equo.*   [10] *Facere impetum.*

[11] *Confertus.* Use superlative. It comes from *con* and *farcio.*

[12] *Triarii.* The Romans generally fought in three lines—hastati, principes, triarii. The best troops were kept in reserve in the third line.

XII. *NEPOS.*

Atticus had an uncle, Q. Cæcilius, a Roman knight, a friend of Lucullus, rich and of a very surly[1] disposition. Cæcilius when dying adopted him by will, and made him heir[2] to three-quarters of his property. From this inheritance he received ten millions[3] of sesterces. He was on intimate[4] terms with Hortensius, who at this time held the foremost place in[5] eloquence, so that it could not be ascertained which[6] of the two loved him most, Cicero who had married[7] his sister, or Hortensius, and what was a most difficult task, he managed[8] that no jealousy[9] should exist between those who had such a rivalry[10] together for renown.—*Atticus,* 5.

---

[1] *Difficilis. Facilis* will express the opposite.

[2] *Hæres ex dodrante. Dodrans (de quadrans,* a quarter off) = three quarters.

[3] *Centies sestertium. Sestertium* is a sum of money equal to 1000 sestertii. When used with numeral adverbs, it means so many hundred thousand sesterces, e.g. *bis sestertium,* 200,000 sesterces.

[4] *Familiariter* or *intime uti aliquo.*

[5] The Latins would say "of."

[6] *Uter.* Mind the sentence is dependent.

[7] *Duco* is used of the man, *nubo* (with dative) of the woman marrying.

[8] *Efficit ut.*

[9] *Obtrectatio.*

[10] *Æmulatio.*

XIII. *CÆSAR.*

Cæsar on the following day sent Labienus his staff-officer[1] with those legions which he had led back from Britain, against the Morini who had rebelled.[2] They, since owing to the dryness[3] of the marshes they had no[4] place to retreat to, almost all fell into the hands of Labienus. But Titurius and Cotta, the staff-officers who had led legions into the territory of the Menapii, after laying waste all their territory, cutting down their corn and burning their buildings, returned to Cæsar because the Menapii had hidden[5] themselves in the thickest woods. Cæsar placed the winter[6] quarters of all his legions among the Belgæ. Two states in the whole of Britain sent hostages there[7]; the rest omitted to do so.— *Bell. Gall.* iv. 38.

---

[1] *Legatus.* Sometimes it means "ambassador." The meaning must be determined by the context.

[2] *Deficio.*

[3] *Siccitas.*

[4] Lit. "they had not where they might retreat."

[5] *Abdo.*

[6] *Hiberna.* The word for summer quarters is *æstiva.* They are really adjectives agreeing with *castra* understood.

[7] *Eo.* Because it means *to* that place; *ibi* means *in* that place.

XIV. *LIVY.*

In Sicily[1] the death of Hiero had changed everything for the Romans, and the sovereignty was transferred to Hieronymus his grandson,[2] a boy who would[3] scarcely bear with moderation liberty, much[4] less absolute[5] power. Such was his age, such was his disposition. Hiero, seeing that this would be the case, is said to have wished in extreme old age to leave Syracuse free, lest the kingdom which had been acquired[6] and strengthened by good[7] policy, should be ruined under the sway of a boy. His daughters opposed[8] this plan of his with all[9] their energy, thinking that the name of king would remain with[10] the boy, but that the management[11] of everything would be in their[10] hands and those of their husbands. Consequently, he only left fifteen guardians[12] of the boy, whom he prayed when dying to[13] maintain the loyalty[14] to the Roman people which had been kept inviolate by him for fifty years.—xxiv. 4.

[1] *Sicilia,* sometimes called *Trinacria* (the place of three promontories).

[2] *Nepos.* What does *nepotism* mean ?   [3] Use future in *rus.*

[4] *Nedum.* Cf. Horace, *Nedum sermonum stet honos et gratia vivax.*

[5] *Dominatio.*   [6] *Partus.*   [7] *Bonæ artes.*

[8] *Obsto,* with dative. It also takes *quominus* after it.

[9] *Summâ ope.*

[10] *Penes* followed by acc. Cf. Ovid, *Me penes est unum vasti custodia mundi.*

[11] *Regimen.*   [12] *Tutor.*   [13] After a verb of praying use *ut.*

[14] *Fides* or *officium.*

XV. *CÆSAR.*

At daybreak[1] all our men had been conveyed across
and the army of the enemy was seen.   Labienus having
exhorted[2] his soldiers to remember their former valour
and numerous victories, and to think that Cæsar himself,
under whose leadership they had often conquered the
enemy, was present in person, gives the signal for[3] the
battle.   On the first onset[4] the enemy are driven back,
and put to flight on[5] the right wing, where the seventh
legion had taken[6] up its position ; on the left wing, which
was[7] held by the twelfth legion, when the first ranks of
the enemy had fallen pierced with javelins, the rest
nevertheless fought like[8] lions, nor did anyone[9] show
symptoms of flight.—*Bell. Gall.* vii. 62.

[1] *Primâ luce.*
[2] *Cohortor.*   Use *ut* after it.
[3] Use the genitive according to Latin idiom.
[4] *Concursus.*
[5] *A dextro cornu.*   Cf. *a tergo, a fronte, a latere.*
[6] *Consisto.*
[7] An English passive may be often well changed into a Latin active.
[8] This is not a Latin expression.   Use *acerrime pugnare.*
[9] *Quisquam,* because all are excluded.   When all are included
use *quivis* or *quilibet.*

XVI. *NEPOS.*

Now Epaminondas, on[1] perceiving that he had received
a deadly wound, and at the same time that if he drew[2]
out the barb which had remained from the spear in his
body he would immediately expire, kept it there until
word[3] was brought back that the Bœotians had conquered.
As soon as he heard that, " I have lived long enough,"
said he, "for I die unconquered." Then having drawn
out the barb he immediately expired. He never married.[4]
When he was censured[5] by Pelopidas, who had a dis-
reputable son, for[6] not leaving children, and when he
(Pelopidas) said that in that he paid[7] no attention to
the interests of his country — "Take care," said he,
"lest you pay less, since[8] you are going to leave behind
you such a son. I shall leave behind the battle of
Leuctra,[9] which must[10] not only survive me, but also live
for ever."—*Epaminondas,* 10.

[1] *Quum* with imperfect subj.

[2] The Latins say, "if he had drawn out," because this would be
prior to his expiring.

[3] *Renuntio.* Use the verb impersonally.

[4] *Duco* (with acc.) is used of the man, *nubo* (with dat.) of the
woman marrying. The Latins also say *dare in matrimonium.*

[5] *Reprehendo.*

[6] *Quod,* with subjunctive or indicative? Cf. Socrates, *Accusatus
est quod juventutem corrumperet.*

[7] *Male consulere alicui.* Note the difference between *consulo te*
and *consulo tibi;* also between *metuo te* and *metuo tibi.*

[8] Use *qui* causal, with subjunctive, of course.

[9] Use an adjective. Cf. *prælium Cannense.*

[10] *Necesse est,* either with infin., *ut* with subjunctive, or subjunctive
without *ut,* e.g. *necesse est ire, ut eam,* or *eam.*

XVII. *CICERO.*

Do you not see how[1] in[2] Homer Nestor very fre-
quently dilates[3] upon his virtues? for he was gazing on
the third generation of men, and[4] had no reason to fear
if he told the truth about himself, that he would appear
too odd[5] or talkative. For, as Homer says, words flowed
from his mouth sweeter than honey; for which sweet-
ness he required[6] no strength of body. And yet Aga-
memnon, the great leader of Greece, nowhere wishes that
he may have ten like Ajax, but like Nestor, and, were
this to happen to him, does not doubt that[7] Troy would
fall in a short time.—*De Senectute*, 31.

---

[1] "How," after a verb of seeing, should be translated by *ut* with
subj.

[2] "In," meaning in an author, should be translated by *apud*. Cf.
Apud Herodotum sunt innumerabiles fabulæ.

[3] *Prædicare de.*

[4] *Nec ei erat verendum.* After a verb of fearing translate "that"
by *ne*, "that not" by *ut.*

[5] *Insolens.* Don't translate this word by "insolent." Cf. *familia,
officium*, etc.

[6] *Egeo.* Find out what cases it governs.

[7] After a verb of doubting translate "that" by *quin* (*qui non*)
with subj.

XVIII. *CÆSAR.*

Many circumstances urged the Gauls to this plan ; the delay [1] of Sabinus during the previous days, the assertion [2] of the deserter, [3] the scarcity of food, for which [4] they had made inadequate provision, the hope from the Venetic war, and because men for the most part readily believe that which they wish.　Induced [5] by these considerations, they do not let Viridorix and the other leaders go from the council until [6] it was granted [7] by them that they should take up arms and hasten to the camp.　On this being granted, joyfully as if victory was assured, [8] after collecting boughs and brushwood [9] with which to fill up the ditches of the Romans, they proceed towards the camp.—*Bell. Gall.* iii. 18.

[1] *Cunctatio.*

[2] *Confirmatio.*

[3] *Transfuga.*

[4] Lit. "for which thing it had been too little carefully provided." The Latins are fond of using a verb impersonally.

[5] *Adductus.*

[6] *Priusquam.*　The *prius* often being in one clause, the *quam* in the next.　It is followed by subj. when any purpose is implied, by indicative when it is merely temporal.

[7] *Concedo.*

[8] *Exploratus.*

[9] *Virgultum.*

XIX. *LIVY.*

When this was reported to Hannibal—for it was not done secretly—he first of all sent men to ͬ summon· Magius to him ² in the camp ; afterwards, when he defiantly ³ refused to come, for that Hannibal had no jurisdiction ⁴ over a Campanian citizen, the Carthaginian fired with anger ordered the man to be arrested ⁵ and brought to him in chains.⁶ Fearing ⁷ then lest some unforeseen disturbance should arise, he himself having ⁸ sent forward a message to Marius Blosius, the Campanian prætor, that he would be at Capua on the next day, sets out from the camp with a small guard. Marius having summoned a meeting, orders ⁹ them to go out in ¹⁰ crowds with their families ¹¹ to ¹² meet Hannibal.—xxiii. 7.

¹ Use *qui* with subjunctive.
² Recollect this "him" refers to the subject.
³ *Ferociter.*
⁴ *Jus in aliquem.*
⁵ *Comprehendo.*
⁶ Literally "bound."
⁷ *Vereor ne.* What does *vereor ut* mean?
⁸ Ablative absolute.
⁹ *Edico.* This verb is followed by *ut.*
¹⁰ *Frequentes.* Cf. *Frequens senatus,* a crowded meeting of the Senate.
¹¹ Don't use *familia,* which means "household ;" say with their wives and children.
¹² *Obviam ire alicui.*

XX. CÆSAR.

On the same day, being informed by the scouts[1] that the enemy had taken up their position at the foot of the mountain eight miles from his[2] camp, he sent men to[3] find out what[4] was the nature of the mountain. They brought[5] back word that the ascent was easy. About[6] the third watch he orders Labienus, his staff-officer,[7] with two legions and those men as guides who had learnt the route, to ascend the highest ridge of the mountain. He shows them what[8] his plan is. He himself, about the fourth watch, hastens by the same[9] route as[9] the enemy had gone towards them, and sends all his cavalry before him. Publius Considius, who was considered most skil-ful[10] in military matters, and had been in the army of Sulla, and afterwards in that of Crassus, is sent forward with scouts.—i. 21.

[1] *Explorator.*
[2] Don't translate here by *ejus.* Why?
[3] Use *qui* with subj.
[4] Use *qualis,* and recollect the sentence is dependent.
[5] *Renuntiare.* Use the verb impersonally.
[6] Use the preposition *de.*
[7] *Legatus.*
[8] Dependent sentence.
[9] *Idem—qui.*
[10] *Rei militaris peritus.*

XXI. *LIVY.*

On the following day a crowded[1] meeting of the Senate was granted to Hannibal. His first speech[2] there was very courteous[3] and kind, in which he thanked[4] the Campanians for having[5] preferred his friendship to the Roman alliance, and among other glorious promises he declared[6] "that in a short time Capua should be the capital of the whole of Italy, and that along with other nations even the Roman people should seek laws from thence. That one man was without[7] share in the Carthaginian friendship and the treaty made with him, who neither was, nor ought to be called a Campanian. Magius Decius. That he demanded his[8] surrender, and that in[9] his presence a motion[10] should be made concerning him, and a decree[11] of the Senate passed."—xxiii. 10.

[1] *Frequens senatus.*
[2] *Oratio.* Recollect *orationem habere* is to make a speech.
[3] *Perblandus.* What force has *per* as a prefix?
[4] *Gratias agere alicui.*
[5] *Quod.*
[6] *Polliceor.* Cf. *ultro polliceor, promitto sæpe rogatus.*
[7] *Exsors* with genitive. Cf. *expers* (*ex pars*).
[8] That he should be given up (*dedo*) to him.
[9] Ablative absolute.
[10] *Referre de aliquo.*
[11] *Senatus Consultum.* Often written shortly, *S. C.*

XXII. *CICERO.*

Yet all cannot be men[1] like Scipio or Maximus, so as to recollect the taking of cities, battles by sea and land, wars that they have waged, triumphs that they have gained. There is also the quiet and mild old age of a life passed tranquilly and with purity and refinement,[2] as we have heard was that of Plato, who died while still writing in his eighty-first year, as was that of Isocrates, who says that he wrote that book which has[3] the title of Panathenaicus in his ninety-fourth year, and he lived five years afterwards. His master Gorgias completed 107 years, nor did he ever flag[4] in his pursuit and work. He,[5] when it was asked[6] of him why[7] he wished to live so long, said, " I have nothing to blame old age for "—a fine answer, and worthy[8] of a learned man.—*De Senectute,* 13.

[1] *Scipiones.*
[2] *Eleganter.*
[3] *Inscribitur.*
[4] *Cesso. Desino* means to cease.
[5] Begin with the relative.
[6] *Quærere ex aliquo.*
[7] This is a dependent clause.
[8] *Dignus* takes the ablative with a noun, and *qui* with subjunctive when used with a verb, e.g. *dignus est qui ametur,* he is worthy to be loved.

XXIII. CÆSAR.

The soldiers of the ninth and tenth legions, when they had taken [1] up their position on the left part of the line, having hurled their javelins,[2] quickly drove from the higher ground into the river the Gauls breathless [3] with running, and pursuing them with their swords as they attempted to cross, slew a great part of them while in [4] difficulties. The soldiers themselves did not hesitate to cross the river, and having advanced to unfavourable ground, on [5] the battle being renewed,[5] put to flight the enemy as they turned back and opposed them. In another part also two different legions, the eleventh and eighth, having [6] routed the Gauls with [7] whom they had engaged,[8] were fighting from the higher ground on the very banks of the river.—*Bell. Gall.* ii. 23.

[1] *Consisto.*
[2] *Pilum.*
[3] *Exanimatus.*
[4] *Impeditus.*
[5] *Redintegro.* Use the abl. abs.
[6] Either abl. abs. or *quum* with the pluperfect subj.
[7] Recollect that when used with the relative or personal pronouns *cum* is enclitic.
[8] *Congredior.*

XXIV. *NEPOS.*

At this time no state came to [1] the assistance of the
Athenians except the Platæans. That state sent a
thousand [2] soldiers. Consequently on their arrival ten
thousand armed men were made [3] up. This force was
fired [4] with a marvellous desire for the fray. The result [5]
was that Miltiades had more influence than his colleagues.
Induced therefore by his influence, the Athenians led out
their forces from the city, and pitched their camp in a
suitable place. Then, on the following day, having drawn [6]
up their army in battle array at the foot of a mountain on
ground not very open, they began the battle with this [7]
design, that they might be protected by the height [8] of
the mountain.—*Miltiades*, 5.

[1] Use double dative. Cf. *Exitio est avidum mare nautis.*

[2] *Mille* may be used either as a substantive or adjective, viz.
mille militum or *mille milites.*

[3] *Compleo.*

[4] *Flagro* (a neuter verb).

[5] *Quo factum est ut* will often be a good translation of "the result
was" or "consequently."

[6] *Aciem instruere.* Note difference between *exercitus* (*exerceo*, to
drill), that which is drilled, *agmen* (for *agimen*), an army on the
march, and *acies*, an army in battle array.

[7] *Eo consilio ut.*

[8] *Altitudo.*

XXV. *CÆSAR.*

The more[1] severe and fierce the siege became day[2] by day, the more[1] numerous despatches and messengers were sent to Cæsar. Some of these being caught, were killed with torture[3] before the eyes of our soldiers. There was within the camp a Nervian, Vertico by name, born in a respectable[4] position, who had fled from the first siege to Cicero, and had plighted[5] him his troth. He persuades[6] a slave by hope of liberty and great rewards to convey a letter to Cæsar. He carries this out fastened[7] to a javelin, and associating[8] as a Gaul among Gauls, without any suspicion reaches Cæsar. From him they[9] learn of the danger of Cicero and the legion.—*Bell. Gall.* v. 45.

[1] *Quanto—tanto.*
[2] *Indies. Quotidie* is used when there is no increase or decrease.
[3] *Cruciatus.*
[4] *Honestus.*
[5] *Fidem præstare alicui.* Cf. the converse *fidem fallere.*
[6] *Persuadeo* takes dative and *ut* with subj.
[7] *Illigatus.*
[8] *Versor.*
[9] Put the verb impersonally.

XXVI. *NEPOS.*

Datames, although he was a long way from those parts, and was[1] called away by more important affairs, yet thought he ought to gratify[2] the wish of the king. Consequently, with a few but brave men, he embarked[3] on board a ship, thinking, as turned out, that he would more easily crush[4] him with a small force when off[5] his guard, than with ever[6] so large an army when prepared. Sailing[7] down in this to Cilicia, after disembarking[8] and marching day and night, he crossed Taurus and reached the[9] place he desired. He inquires where[10] Aspis is; he finds out that he was not far off, and that he had gone to[11] hunt. While he considers[12] this, the reason of his arrival is discovered. Aspis gets the Pisidians along with those whom he had with him to[13] offer resistance. When Datames heard this, he takes his arms and orders his men to follow. He himself, at[14] full speed, rushes on the foe.—*Datames*, 4.

---

[1] *Abstraho.*
[2] *Morem gerere alicui.*
[3] *Conscendere navem.* So *conscendere equum.*
[4] *Opprimo.*   [5] *Imprudens.*
[6] *Quamvis magnus.*   [7] *Hac delatus.*
[8] *Egredior.*   [9] *Eo quo studuerat venit.*
[10] This is a dependent sentence.
[11] Supine in *um.* This is used after verbs of motion.
[12] *Speculor.*
[13] Not the infinitive, but *ad resistendum.*
[14] *Equo concitato* or *equo admisso* (Cæsar).

XXVII. *CÆSAR.*

In that battle seventy-four of our cavalry were killed ; among them Piso, a very brave man, of very high birth, whose grandfather[1] had held[2] sovereign power in his state, having[3] the title of friend given him by our Senate. He bearing[4] aid to his brother when cut[5] off by the enemy, rescued him from danger, but being himself pitched[6] from his wounded horse, resisted as long as he could. When after[7] receiving many wounds he had been surrounded and slain, his brother, who had by this time retired from the battle, perceived it from a distance, and, spurring[8] his horse, rushed upon the enemy and was slain.—*Bell. Gall.* iv. 12.

[1] *Avus.* The order is *pater, avus, proavus, abavus, atavus.* Cf. *Mæcenas atavis edite regibus.*

[2] *Obtineo.* Don't translate this verb by " obtain."

[3] *Appellatus.* All verbs of being called are copulative.

[4] Avoid a present participle, and use *quum* with imperfect subj.

[5] *Intercludo.*

[6] *Dejectus.*

[7] Abl. abs.

[8] *Equo incitato* or *calcaribus subditis.*

XXVIII. *SALLUST.*

As[1] soon as after the division of the kingdom the ambassadors had departed from Africa, and Jugurtha, contrary to his fears, saw that he had[2] obtained the rewards of his guilt, thinking it certain, as[3] he had heard from his friends at Numantia, that everything had[4] its price at Rome, at the same time also fired by the promises of those whom a short time previously he had loaded[5] with gifts, he fixed[6] his thoughts on the kingdom of Adherbal.   He himself was fierce and warlike ; but he who[7] was the object of his attack was quiet and unwarlike, of a peaceful nature, suitable for wrong, rather fearing than to be feared.   Therefore he unexpectedly[8] invades his territory with a great force, captures many men, with cattle and other booty, burns the buildings, then returns with all his host[9] to his own kingdom, thinking that Adherbal, roused by the wrong, would avenge[10] his wrongs by force, and that that would be a ground of war.—*Jugurtha,* 20.

[1] *Postquam* never means afterwards, which is *post* or *postea.*
[2] *Adipiscor.*
[3] " A thing which," *quod.*
[4] *Venalis,* whence our word "venal."
[5] *Expleo.*
[6] *Intendere animum.*
[7] *Quem petebat.*
[8] *De* or *ex improviso.*
[9] *Multitudo.*
[10] *Vindico.*

XXIX. *CÆSAR.*

On the following day the general, having[1] called a council, points out that he had undertaken[2] that war not for the sake of his own needs, but for the sake of the common safety, and since[3] he must bow[4] to fate, that he offered himself to them for either purpose, whether they wished by his death to satisfy the Romans or to[5] give him up alive. Ambassadors are sent to Cæsar touching[6] these matters. He orders the arms to be given up and the chiefs to be brought to him. When he had taken his seat on the fortification before the camp, the chiefs are brought there,[7] and by Cæsar's orders beheaded,[8] because they had attempted a revolution.[9]—*Bell. Gall.* vii. 89.

[1] Use either the abl. abs. or *quum* with the pluperfect subj.

[2] *Suscipio.*

[3] *Quoniam*, followed here by subjunctive, because it is what he said.

[4] *Cedere fato.*

[5] *Trado* or *transdo.*

[6] *De.*

[7] *Eo* = there, to that place ; *ibi* = there, in that place.

[8] *Securi ferire* (lit. to strike with an axe).

[9] *Res novæ. Res nova* = a novelty.

XXX. *LIVY.*

Camillus orders his countrymen to throw their baggage[1] into a heap, to get ready their army, and to regain[2] their country with the sword and not with gold, having in their sight the temples of the gods, their wives and children, and the soil of their country disfigured[3] by the evils of war. Then he draws[4] up his army, as the nature of the place allowed, on the site of the half-ruined[5] city, and secured[6] all things which could be chosen or prepared advantageous[7] for his own men. The Gauls, alarmed by the new[8] state of affairs, take up arms; under the influence of anger rather than design, they rush upon the Romans. Now Fortune had changed; now the power of the gods and the plans of men aided the Roman[9] cause. Therefore at the first onset the Gauls were routed with no greater difficulty[10] than they had conquered at the Allia.—v. 49.

[1] *Sarcinæ. Impedimenta* means the heavy baggage of an army.
[2] *Recuperare.*
[3] *Deformis.*
[4] *Instruere aciem.*
[5] *Semirutus.*
[6] *Provideo.*
[7] *Secundus.* Cf. *res secundæ, secundo flumine.*
[8] *Nova res. Novæ res* means a revolution.
[9] *Res Romana.*
[10] *Momentum.*

XXXI. *CICERO.*

When Damocles said that no man was ever more blessed than him (Dionysius), "Do you wish," said he, "O Damocles, since this life delights you, to taste the same and to make trial of my fortune." On[3] his saying that he desired it, he ordered the man to be placed on a gilded couch. Then he commanded chosen slaves of remarkable[4] beauty to stand at the table and carefully to[5] wait upon him. Perfumes[6] and garlands were there; the tables were loaded[7] with most sumptuous[8] viands. Damocles thought himself happy. In the midst of this splendour[9] Dionysius ordered a glittering sword, fastened to the ceiling[10] by a horse-hair, to be let down so as to hang[11] over his neck. Consequently he neither regarded those beautiful attendants, nor did he stretch out his hand towards the table. At last he begged the tyrant that he might depart, since[12] he no longer wished to be happy.—*Tusc. Quæst.* v. 21.

---

[1] Use *nego.* Cf. *Nego hæc vera esse* = I say that this is not true.
[2] *Degustare.*
[3] Use *quum* with pluperfect subj.
[4] *Eximius.* Use ablative of quality.
[5] *Ministrare.*   [6] *Unguenta.*   [7] *Exstruo.*
[8] *Conquisitus.*   [9] *Apparatus.*   [10] *Lacunar.*
[11] *Impendeo* with dative.
[12] *Quod,* followed by subjunctive, because it is what he said.

XXXII. *CÆSAR.*

Cæsar, being[1] informed by Titurius, leads across a bridge all his cavalry and the Numidians of light armour,[2] slingers and archers, and hastens towards them. A[3] fierce fight took place there. The enemy attacking our men when in[4] difficulties, slew a great number of them. They drove back with a shower[5] of missiles the remainder when they most valiantly endeavoured to cross on their bodies. They surrounded[6] with their cavalry, and killed the first who had crossed. The enemy, when they perceived that their hopes of[7] taking the town and crossing the river had disappointed[8] them, and saw that our men were not advancing to more unfavourable ground for the purpose of fighting, having convened a council, determined that it was best for each man to return to his home.[9]—*Bell. Gall.* ii. 10.

[1] *Certior factus.* The construction is *aliquem certiorem facere de.*
[2] *Armatura.*
[3] Say "it was fought fiercely." The Latins often use a verb impersonally.
[4] *Impeditus* (*in* and *pes*). The opposite word is *expeditus.*
[5] *Multitudo.*
[6] Instead of two perfects, say "they killed surrounded."
[7] Use *de* with gerundives.
[8] *Fallo.* It also means "to escape the notice of."
[9] *Domus, humus,* and *rus* imitate the construction of towns.

XXXIII. *SALLUST.*

O conscript fathers, my father Micipsa when[1] dying enjoined[2] me to consider that the administration[3] only of the kingdom of Numidia was mine, that in[4] all other respects the authority and sovereignty of it were in[5] your hands ; at the same time to strive to be of[6] the greatest use to the Roman people at[7] home and abroad ; to consider you in the light[8] of relations by blood ; (saying) if I did so that I should have in your friendship an army and wealth, the bulwarks[9] of a kingdom. While I was prosecuting[10] these precepts of my father, Jugurtha, a man the most wicked of all whom the earth puts up with, despising[11] your sovereignty, banished me, the grandson of Masinissa, the ally and friend of the Roman people, from my kingdom and possessions.—*Jugurtha,* 14.

[1] The pres. participle or *quum* with subjunctive.
[2] *Præcipio,* with dative, followed by *ut.*
[3] *Procuratio.*
[4] *Ceterum.*
[5] *Penes vos esse.*
[6] The Latins use the dative. Cf. *exitio est avidum mare nautis.*
[7] *Domi militiæque.*
[8] *Locus* will translate "light" in this sense.
[9] *Munimenta.*
[10] *Agito.*
[11] Use abl. abs.

XXXIV. *CÆSAR.*

Startled[1] by this news and despatch, Cæsar enrolled[2] two new legions in Hither[3] Gaul, and at the commencement of summer sent Q. Pedius, his staff-officer, to lead them into the interior of Gaul. He himself, as soon as there began to be plenty of fodder,[4] came to the army. He commissions[5] the Senones and the other Gauls who were neighbours of the Belgæ to find out what was going on among them, and to inform him of these matters. All of them uniformly[6] brought back word that bands were collecting, and that an army was assembling at one place. Then, indeed, he thought he ought not to hesitate[7] to march against them. Having[8] seen to his corn supply, he strikes his camp, and in about fifteen days reaches[9] the territory of the Belgæ.—ii. 2.

[1] *Commoveo.*
[2] *Conscribo.*   Hence our word "conscription."
[3] *Citerior*, i.e. on the Roman side of the Alps.
[4] *Pabulum.*
[5] *Dare negotium.*
[6] *Constanter.*
[7] *Dubito.*   Use *quin* after it.
[8] "Having" may generally be put into Latin by *quum* with the pluperfect subj., or the abl. abs.
[9] *Pervenire ad.*

XXXV. *CICERO.*

The story of Cleobis and Biton, sons of a priestess at Argos, is well known. For when it was right that she should be carried in a chariot to a solemn and appointed sacrifice to a temple a considerable[1] distance from the town and the beasts[2] of burden delayed,[3] then those youths whom I have lately mentioned, having[4] doffed their robes, anointed[5] their bodies with oil and approached the yoke. When the priestess reached the temple, since the chariot had been drawn by her sons, she is said to have prayed[6] the goddess to give them in return for their filial[7] love the greatest reward that could be given by a god to man. That afterwards the young[8] men, having banqueted with their mother, consigned[9] themselves to sleep. That in the morning they were found dead.— *Tusc. Disput.* i. 47.

---

[1] *Satis longe.*

[2] *Jumentum.*

[3] *Moror. Nil moror* means " I care nothing for."

[4] *Ponere vestem.* Use abl. abs.

[5] *Perunguo.*

[6] *Precor ut,* or with a negative, *ne.*

[7] *Pietas.* Also means *loyalty, religion.*

[8] *Juvenis* is a man up to forty-five, *adolescens,* a youth in our sense.

[9] *Do.*

XXXVI. *CÆSAR.*

The Germans hearing[1] shouts in the rear and seeing[2] their men being killed, having thrown away their arms and left the military standards, rushed from the camp. When they had reached the confluence[3] of the Meuse and the Rhine, despairing[1] of further flight, a great number having been killed, the remainder threw[4] them-selves headlong into the river, and overpowered by weariness and the force of the river, perished.   Our soldiers, all safe to[5] a man, returned to the camp. Cæsar gave those whom he had kept in the camp the opportunity[6] of departing ; but they, fearing punishment and torture[7] from the Gauls whose territory they had laid waste, said they preferred to remain with him. Cæsar granted them freedom.—*Bell. Gall.* iv. 15.

[1] Abl. abs.

[2] *Quum,* with imperfect subj.

[3] *Confluens.*

[4] *Se præcipitare.*

[5] *Ad unum.*

[6] *Potestas.*   Opportunity may often be translated by *occasio* or *facultas.*

[7] *Cruciatus Gallorum.*   This means, according to the context, either the torture inflicted *on* or *by* the Gauls.   In the former case *Gallorum* is the objective, in the latter the subjective genitive.

XXXVII. *NEPOS.*

When he was of great age and had ceased[1] to hold office, the Athenians began[2] to be hard pressed in war on all sides. Samos had revolted, the Hellespont had[3] gone over, and Philip the Macedonian, even then powerful, was forming[4] many plans. Chares was opposed to him, and was not thought to afford sufficient[5] protection. It[6] is decreed, therefore, that Menestheus, son of Iphicrates and son-in-law of Timotheus, should set out to the war. To[7] advise him are given two men pre-eminent in experience[8] and wisdom, viz. his father and father-in-law, because they possessed such great influence that there was a confident hope that by their means what was lost might be recovered.[9] When they had set out for Samos, and Chares, on learning their approach, was setting out for the same place with his forces, that[10] nothing might seem to be done in[11] his absence, it[12] happened that as they were approaching the island a great storm arose.— *Timotheus,* 3.

---

[1] *Desino. Cesso* does not mean to cease, but to flag.
[2] Before a passive infin. use *captus sum.*   [3] *Descisco.*
[4] *Multa moliri. Molior* is a verb signifying effort; it is used in Virgil in several expressions, e.g. *moliri bipennem, moliri arcem, moliri habenas.*
[5] *Satis* with genitive.   [6] *Decerno.* This verb is followed by *ut.*
[7] *Huic in consilium dantur.*   [8] *Usus.*   [9] *Recuperare.*
[10] *Ne quid* with a purpose, *ut nihil* with a consequence.
[11] Ablative absolute.
[12] *Accidit ut.* So *sequitur, restat, fit,* are followed by *ut.*

XXXVIII. *LIVY.*

Never was the same nature more adapted [1] for very
different ends,[2] obeying [3] and commanding.   Consequently, you could not easily determine whether [4] he
were more dear to the commander-in-chief or to the army.
Neither did Hasdrubal prefer to put any other in command whenever [5] anything had to be done with bravery [6]
or energy,[6] nor did the soldiers have more confidence in
any other leader. He had the greatest bravery in [7] risking
danger, the greatest [8] tact when in the thick of it.
Neither could his body be wearied, nor his spirits subdued by any hardship.   He [9] could equally endure heat
and cold.   His times for waking [10] and sleeping were distinguished [11] neither by day nor night. What [12] remained
after the transaction of business was given to rest.   That
was courted [13] neither by a soft bed nor by silence.
Many often saw him wrapped up in his military [14] coat
lying on the ground mid the guards and pickets of the
soldiers.—xxi. 4.

---

[1] *Habilis.*   [2] *Res.*   [3] Use the gerund.

[4] *Utrum—an, num—an, ne—an,—an, —ne* are used in a dependent sentence.

[5] This being indefinite the subjunctive must be used.

[6] Use adverbs.   [7] *Ad pericula capessenda.*

[8] Use *plurimum* with genitive after it.

[9] Lit. "There was an equal endurance."   [10] *Vigiliæ.*

[11] *Discrimino.*   [12] *Id quod rebus gerendis superesset* (indefinite).

[13] *Accerso* or *arcesso*, two different forms.   [14] *Sagulum.*

[XXXIX. *NEPOS.*]

Phocion the Athenian, although he often commanded armies and held very high offices, is yet better known for his uprightness² than for his exertions in³ war. The recollection, therefore, of the latter⁴ is lost, while his reputation for the former¹ is great, in consequence of which he had given⁵ him the title of the Good. For he was continually poor, though he might have been very rich, owing to the many offices entrusted⁶ to him and the high commands which were given him by the people. When he refused⁷ the gift of a large sum of money sent by King Philip, and the ambassadors exhorted him to receive it, and at the same time advised him, if he himself could easily do⁸ without it, that he should yet provide for his children, since⁹ they would find it difficult in very great poverty to maintain the great position¹⁰ of their father, "if they are like me," said he, "this small¹¹ estate which has brought me to this position will maintain them, but if they are going to be unlike, I am unwilling that their luxury should be fostered and increased at¹² my expense."

(—*Phocion.*)

¹ *Quum, quamvis, licet, quanquam, etsi* all mean "although." The first three are followed by subjunctive, the last two by indicative.

² *Integritas* (*in* and *tango*). Cf. Horace, *integer vitæ scelerisque purus.*

³ The Latins use the genitive where we don't; so here *labor rei militaris.* Cf. *tempestas maris*, a storm *at* sea.

⁴ *Hic* the latter, *ille* the former.

⁵ *Appellor.* Verbs of being called are of course copulative and take the same case after as before them.

⁶ *Defero.*   ⁷ *Recuso* or *repudio.*

⁸ *Careo* with abl. Cf. *carmina sola carent fato.*

⁹ Use *qui* with subjunctive.

¹⁰ *Dignitas.*   ¹¹ *Agellus.*   ¹² *Meis impensis.*

XL. CÆSAR.

Put into Oratio obliqua.

Ambiorix said, " I admit that in [1] return for Cæsar's kindness towards me I [2] owe him a deep debt of gratitude, because by his agency [3] I have been freed from the tax which I was accustomed to pay to the Aduatuci my neighbours, and because my son and nephew, whom the Aduatuci kept among them in slavery and chains, have been sent back to me by Cæsar. Nor did I do that which I did do about attacking the camp either by my own judgment or wish, but by compulsion [4] of the state, and my authority is of [5] such a kind that the people have no less power over me than I have over the people. Furthermore, the cause of war to the state was this, that it was unable to resist a sudden conspiracy of the Gauls. I can easily prove this by my weakness, [6] for I am not so devoid [7] of common sense as to think that I can conquer the Roman people with my forces."—*Bell. Gall.* v. 27.

[1] *Pro.*
[2] *Plurimum alicui debere.*
[3] *Opera.*
[4] *Coactu.*
[5] *Ejusmodi ut.*
[6] *Humilitas.*
[7] *Imperitus rerum.*

XLI. SALLUST.

Jugurtha, when he thought that they had departed from Africa, and found that owing to the nature of the ground he was unable to[1] take Cirta by[1] assault, surrounds[2] the walls with a rampart[3] and ditch, erects towers, and strengthens them with garrisons. Furthermore, by day and night he assails[4] them either by force or treachery, at one time displaying[5] before the defenders of the walls rewards, at another time (cause for) fear. When Adherbal perceived that his fate[6] is critical, that the enemy is advancing, that there is no hope of aid, that for[7] want of necessaries the war cannot be prolonged,[8] of those who had fled together to Cirta he selects two who were especially active ; by making them great promises, and by deploring his lot, he persuades them to proceed by night through the[9] lines of the enemy to the nearest part of the sea, and then to Rome.—*Jugurtha*, 23.

[1] *Expugnare* or *per vim expugnare.*

[2] *Circumdo* has two constructions, e.g. *circumdo urbem muro* or *circumdo murum urbi.*

[3] *Vallum. Vallus* means a palisade.

[4] *Tempto.* Use historical infinitive.

[5] *Ostento.* This is the frequentative of *ostendo.*

[6] *Fortunas in extremo sitas.*

[7] Ablative of cause.

[8] *Traho* or *duco.*

[9] *Munitiones.*

XLII. *CICERO.*

On the day after that day when I[1] was intending to set
out from Athens, about the tenth hour of the night
Postumius came to me and told me that Marcellus our
colleague had been struck with a dagger[2] after dinner[3] by
Magius his friend, and had received two wounds, one in
the stomach, the other on the head by[4] the ear; that he
hoped, however, that he could live. That Magius had
killed[5] himself; that afterwards he had been sent to me
by Marcellus to[6] tell me this, and to[6] ask me to collect
doctors. I collected them, and I immediately[7] set out
there[8] at daybreak.[9] When I was not far from the
Piræus a slave met[10] me with a note,[11] in which it was
written that Marcellus had died[12] a little before dawn.—
Ep. ad Div. iv. 12.

[1] *In animo habere.* Cf. *mihi est in animo.*
[2] *Pugio.* Mark the gender.
[3] *Cœna* (κοίνος), properly the common meal of the day.
[4] *Secundum*, a preposition governing acc.
[5] *Se interficere* or *mortem sibi consciscere.*
[6] Use *qui* with subjunctive.
[7] *E vestigio.*
[8] Ask yourself if it means *to* that place or *in* that place.
[9] *Primâ luce.*
[10] *Obviam ire* with dat.
[11] *Codicilli.*
[12] *Diem suum obire.*

XLIII. *CÆSAR.*

When this opinion was approved by the consent of all, on one day more[1] than twenty cities are set on fire. This same thing is done in the other states. Fires are seen in all directions. Though all were greatly[2] annoyed at this, they yet set before them so much consolation that they were sure, since victory was almost assured,[3] that they would quickly recover[4] what they had lost. They[5] deliberate at a common council about Avaricum, whether[6] it pleased it should be burnt or defended. The inhabitants threw[7] themselves at the feet of the Gauls, begging that they might not be compelled with their own hands to set on fire almost the most beautiful city of the whole of Gaul, which was the bulwark[8] and pride of the state. They say that they will easily defend it, because,[9] being surrounded on almost all sides by a river and marsh, it has (but) one very narrow approach.—*Bell. Gall.* vii. 15.

[1] *Amplius.* The *quam* is often omitted.
[2] Cf. *Ægre ferre aliquid.* The opposite is *æquo animo ferre.*
[3] *Exploratus.*
[4] *Recuperare.*
[5] Put the verb impersonally.
[6] In dependent sentences use *utrum—an,* or *num—an,* or *ne—an,* or—*ne,* or—*an.*
[7] *Projicere se ad pedes alicui.*
[8] *Propugnaculum.*
[9] *Quod.* Followed here by subjunctive, because it does not state a fact, but what they said.

XLIV. *NEPOS.*

Now Chabrias perished in the following manner.
The Athenians were attacking Chios. Chabrias was in
the fleet in[1] a private capacity, but he surpassed in influence[2] all who[3] were in authority, and the soldiers
looked to him more than to those who were in command.
This circumstance hastened his death. For while he is
anxious[4] to[5] be the first to enter the harbour, and orders
his pilot[6] to guide his ship there,[7] he[8] proved his own
destruction. For when he had entered there the other
ships did not follow. On this happening, while he was
fighting like[9] a lion, surrounded by the enemy, his ship
being struck by a ram[10] began to[11] sink. Though he
might have escaped from here by[12] throwing himself into
the sea, since the fleet of the Athenians was near to[13]
pick up the swimmers, he preferred to perish rather than
to[14] throw away his arms and leave the ship in which he
had been borne.—*Chabrias*, 4.

---

[1] *Privatus.*   [2] *Auctoritas.*   [3] *Qui in magistratu erant.*

[4] *Studet.*   [5] Cf. *Primus hoc feci*, I was the first to do this.

[6] *Gubernator.*

[7] *Eo* = there, to that place ; *ibi* = there, in that place.

[8] Use a double dative. Cf. *exitio est avidum mare nautis.*

[9] The Latins say *acerrime* or *fortissime pugnare.*

[10] *Rostrum*, properly the beak of the ship.

[11] *Sidere.*

[12] Say " if he had thrown," &c.

[13] *Quæ exciperet.*

[14] Use an ablative absolute.

XLV. *SALLUST.*

The Roman commander, when he saw that he was being wearied[1] out by stratagems, and that no opportunity[2] of fighting was given by the enemy, determined to attack a great city, the stronghold[3] of the kingdom in that part where it was situated, by name Zama, thinking that Jugurtha would come to[4] the assistance of his countrymen in[5] their difficulties, and that a battle would take place there. But he, being informed by deserters[6] what was being prepared, anticipated[7] Metellus by forced[8] marches, exhorted[9] the townspeople to defend the walls, having added some deserters to[4] protect the place; furthermore, he promised[10] that he himself would be present in time with an army.—*Jugurtha,* 56.

[1] *Fatigo.*
[2] *Copia pugnandi fit.*
[3] *Arx.*
[4] Use *dativus propositi.*
[5] *Laborare* means "to be in difficulties."
[6] *Perfuga.*
[7] *Antevenio.*
[8] *Magnum iter.*
[9] Cf. *Hortor te ut hoc facias.*
[10] After a verb of promising use future infinitive. Also distinguish between *polliceor* and *promitto.* Cf. *ultro polliceor ; promitto sæpe rogatus.*

XLVI. *CICERO.*

When Pyrrhus had made [1] war on the Roman people, and when there was a struggle for empire with a king generous and powerful, a deserter [2] came from him to the camp of Fabricius and promised him, if he [3] would give him a reward, that he would return to the camp of Pyrrhus with the same secresy that he had come, and would kill him by poison. Fabricius took care [4] that he should be taken back to Pyrrhus, and that action of his was commended by the Senate. Yet, [5] if we look to the appearance and the notion of expediency, [6] one deserter would have done away with that war and a dangerous foe to the empire, but it would have been a great disgrace [7] that he with [8] whom there had been a contest for renown should be overpowered, not by valour, but by poison.—*De Off.* iii. 22.

[1] *Inferre bellum alicui.*

[2] *Perfuga.*

[3] Literally, "if he had given him," because the giving would precede the deed.

[4] *Curo,* generally followed by gerundive, e.g. *curabo pontem faciendum.*

[5] *Atqui.*

[6] *Utilitas.*

[7] *Dedecus.*

[8] Instead of *quocum* the Latins often use *quicum.*

XLVII. *NEPOS.*

Pausanias fled for refuge to the temple [1] of Minerva. That [2] he might not be able to get out from there, the Ephors [3] immediately blocked [4] up the folding [5] doors of that temple, and demolished the roof that [6] he might the more quickly perish under [7] the open sky. It is said that the mother of Pausanias was alive at that time, and that she, now advanced [8] in years, as soon as she learnt her son's guilt, among the first brought a stone to the entrance of the temple to shut in her son. Thus Pausanias sullied [9] by an ignominious death his great fame in [10] war. Having been carried half [11] dead out of the temple, he immediately breathed [12] his last. Though several said that his dead body ought to be taken to the same place as [13] those who had suffered punishment, it found [14] no favour with the majority, and they buried him at a distance from that place where he had died.—*Pausanias,* 5.

[1] *Ædes* in the singular. Synonyms are *templum, fanum, delubrum.*

[2] Observe this is a purpose.

[3] Ephorus (a body of five magistrates at Sparta).

[4] *Obstruo.*   [5] *Valvæ.*

[6] Use *quo* instead of *ut* where there is a comparative.

[7] *Sub Divo.*   [8] *Grandis natu* or *ætate provectus.*

[9] *Maculo.* Cf. our "immaculate."

[10] The Latins would say "of war."

[11] *Semianimis.*   [12] *Animam efflare.*

[13] Recollect *idem—qui.* Here *eodem—quo.*

[14] *Displicuit.*

XLVIII. *CICERO.*

But why do I mention those things? A slave of Clodius, whom he had placed to[1] kill Cneius Pompey, was arrested[2] in the temple of Castor. The dagger[3] was wrested[4] from his hands as he confessed it! Pompey afterwards kept[5] away from the forum, kept away from the senate; he protected himself by his gate and walls,[6] not by the authority of laws or judicial[7] procedures. Was[8] any[9] bill[10] proposed? Was any inquiry voted? Yet if the circumstance, if the man, if any occasion was worthy of it, at any rate all these things were very great in that case. The assassin[11] was posted in the forum and in the very portico[12] of the Senate; death,[13] moreover, was designed against that man on whose life the safety of the state depended.[14]—*Pro Milone,* 7.

[1] Use *ad* with gerundive.
[2] *Comprehendo.*
[3] *Sica* (*secica* from *seco*).
[4] *Extorqueo* followed by dative of person.   Cf. *eripio librum tibi.*
[5] *Careo.*
[6] *Paries* is the word for the wall of a house.
[7] *Judicia.*
[8] The answer *no* is evidently expected, therefore use *num.*
[9] After *num, si, nisi, ne,* translate *any* by *quis.*
[10] *Rogatio lata est.*
[11] *Insidiator.*
[12] *Vestibulum.*
[13] Lit. "was being prepared for that man."
[14] To depend on, *niti in.*

XLIX. *CÆSAR.*

While [1] this was going on Labienus, having left at Agendicum that reinforcement [2] which had lately come from Italy to guard the baggage, [3] sets out for Paris [4] with four legions. This is a town of the Parisii, situated on an island of the river Seine. [5] On his approach being known by the enemy, great forces assembled from the neighbouring states. The chief [6] command is given to Camulogenus, who, though almost worn [7] out with age, was yet summoned to this office [8] owing to his marvellous knowledge of military affairs. He having noticed that there was a marsh which drained [9] into the Seine, took up his position there, and determined to stop our men from crossing. Labienus at first endeavoured to move up the pent-houses, [10] to fill up the marsh with hurdles [11] and earth, and to make [12] a road. But when he perceived that this was done with difficulty, setting out in silence from the camp at the third watch, he reached Melodunum by the same [13] route that [13] he had come.— *Bell. Gall.* vii. 57.

[1] *Dum*, meaning while, is generally followed by a present.
[2] *Supplementum.*
[3] *Impedimenta* is the heavy baggage, *sarcinæ* the soldiers' baggage.
[4] *Lutetia.*   [5] *Sequana.*   [6] *Summa imperii.*
[7] *Confectus.*
[8] *Honor*, like the Greek τιμή, often means office.
[9] *Influo.*   [10] *Vinea.*   [11] *Crates.*
[12] *Munire viam.*   [13] *Idem—qui.*

E

L. *NEPOS.*

He waged war with the Thracians. He restored Seuthes, the ally of the Athenians, to his kingdom. At Corinth he commanded [1] the army with such [2] sternness that never in Greece were any forces better [3] drilled or more obedient [4] to orders, and he brought them to such a state of practice, [5] that when the signal for battle was given by the commander-in-chief, they took [6] their place in such order without the aid of their captain, that they seemed placed [7] in their several positions by a most skilled commander. With this force he slew a regiment [8] of Lacedæmonians. A second time in the same war he put [9] to rout all their forces, by which exploit he acquired [10] great renown. When Artaxerxes wished to [11] make war on the King of Egypt, he asked the Athenians for Iphicrates as general to [12] put in command of his mercenary force.—*Iphicrates*, 2.

[1] *Præsum*, with dative, to command ; *præficio*, with acc. (of person) and dative, to put in command of.

[2] *Tantus—ut* or *is—ut*.

[3] *Exercitatiores.*   [4] *Dicto audientes.*

[5] *Consuetudo.*   [6] *Consisto.*

[7] *Dispono* is used of the placing of troops.

[8] *Mora.* Among the Romans it was *cohors.*

[9] *Fugo.* Observe the difference between this verb and *fugio*, to flee.

[10] *Adipiscor.*   [11] *Inferre bellum alicui.*

[12] You can't use infinitive. Translate, " whom he might put," etc.

LI. *SALLUST.*

When this letter [1] had been read, there [2] were some who gave [3] their opinion that an army should be sent into Africa, and that Adherbal should be assisted [4] as soon as possible; that meanwhile they should deliberate about Jugurtha, since [5] he had not obeyed the ambassadors. But those same supporters [6] of the king struggled [7] in every way that such a decree should not pass. Thus the public good, as usually happens in most matters, was overpowered by private influence. [8] Nevertheless, there are sent as ambassadors to Africa old men of noble birth who had filled [9] the highest offices. Among these was Scaurus, whom we have mentioned above, a man of consular rank and then chief of the Senate.—*Jugurtha,* 25.

[1] *Litteræ* in the plural. *Littera* means a letter of the alphabet.
[2] *Sunt qui* is followed by subjunctive.
[3] To give an official opinion is *censeo.*
[4] "That it should be assisted to." Use *subvenio.* When a verb governs the dative in the active it is used impersonally in the passive. Cf. *mihi persuadebitur,* I shall be persuaded.
[5] *Quoniam* here expresses what they said, and is therefore followed by subjunctive.
[6] *Fautor,* substantive of *faveo.*
[7] It was struggled (*enisum est*) by.
[8] Not *influentia,* which is a barbarism, but *gratia.*
[9] *Uti amplissimis honoribus.*

LII. *NEPOS.*

That [1] they might the more easily repel them if by
chance they attempted to renew the war, Aristides was
chosen to [2] fix how [3] much money each state should give
to [4] build fleets and prepare armies, and by his decision
460 talents were paid [5] in to Delos. For they wished
that to be the public treasury. [6] All this [7] money was
afterwards transferred to Athens. There is no more
certain proof of the self-restraint [2] of this man than the
fact that, though [9] he had held such important commands,
he died in such great poverty that he scarcely left
enough [10] to be buried with. The result [11] was that his
daughters were brought up at the public expense, and
were given [12] in marriage with dowries paid out of the
public treasury. Now he died about four years after
Themistocles had been banished from Athens.—
Aristides, 3.

[1] Where there is a comparative use *quo* instead of *ut.*
[2] Use *qui* with subjunctive.
[3] Observe this is a dependent sentence.
[4] Use *ad* with the gerundive.   [5] *Confero.*
[6] *Ærarium. Fiscus* means private purse of emperor.
[7] Begin with relative.
[8] *Abstinentia.* Say, " of what self-restraint he was."
[9] *Quum* with subjunctive. *Licet* and *quamvis* are also followed by
subjunctive, *etsi* and *quanquam* by indicative.
[10] With what he might be buried (*effero*).
[11] A good translation is always *quo factum est ut.*
[12] *Collocare.* Recollect *duco* is used of the man, *nubo* of the woman
marrying.

LIII. *SALLUST.*

Don't[1] imagine that our ancestors made the state
great from small by arms. If[2] that were so, we should
now have a state by far the fairest ; for we have a greater
supply of allies and citizens, furthermore of arms and
horses, than they had. But there were other qualities
which made them great, which[3] for us have no existence,
diligence at home, a just government abroad,[4] minds
free in deliberation, neither under[5] the influence of
crime nor passion.[6] Instead of these we have luxury and
avarice, poverty in[7] the state, wealth in[7] individuals ; we
eulogize riches, we court inactivity[8] ; between good and
bad there is no distinction[9] ; ambition possesses all the
rewards of virtue. But I pass over these things. Most
noble citizens have conspired to burn their country ; they
summon[10] to their aid the nation of the Gauls most
hostile to the Roman name ; the general of the enemy
with his army is over your head. Do you even now
hesitate and doubt what[11] to do to the enemies whom
you have caught within the walls?[12]—*Catiline,* lii. 19.

[1] Use imperative of *nolo.* Cf. *noli hoc facere.*
[2] Cf. *si quid haberem* (which I have not) *darem.*
[3] Which for us are nothing (*nullus*).   [4] *Foris.*
[5] *Obnoxius,* followed by dative.
[6] *Lubido.*   [7] *Publice—privatim.*   [8] *Inertia.*
[9] *Discrimen.* This word may often be translated "danger."
[10] *Arcesso.*   [11] A dependent sentence.
[12] *Mœnia. Murus* is a general word. *Paries* is always the
wall of a house.

LIV. *NEPOS.*

Hannibal kept himself in one place, in a fort which had been given him by the king as[1] a gift, and he had so[2] built it that it had outlets[3] on all sides, fearing,[4] forsooth,[5] that that would happen which did happen. When the ambassadors of the Roman people had come here,[6] and had surrounded his abode with a great number of soldiers, a slave looking out from a door told[7] Hannibal that several armed men appeared. He ordered[8] him to go round all the doors of the building and quickly bring him back word whether[9] it was beset[10] in the same manner on all sides. When the slave had quickly brought back word that all the outlets were guarded,[11] he perceived that this had not happened by chance, but that[12] he was their object and that[13] he could no longer retain his life.—*Hannibal*, 12.

---

[1] The Latins say, *dono dare aliquid.*

[2] *Sic* or *ita*, followed by *ut.*　　　　[3] *Exitus.*

[4] *Vereor.* Mind the difference in using *ne* or *ut* after it.

[5] *Scilicet* (*scire licet*, you may know).

[6] Not *hic*, which means *in* this place, but *huc.*

[7] Not *dixit Hannibalem*, but *Hannibali.*

[8] *Impero.* Construction, dative case and *ut* with subjunctive.

[9] *Num.* Not *seu, sive, vel*, or *aut* in a dependent sentence.

[10] *Obsideo.*　　　　[11] *Occupo.*

[12] Lit. that he was sought.

[13] Lit. nor that life any longer was to be retained by him. Mind the participle in *dus* is followed by the dative.

LV. *LIVY.*

" Consequently you must[1] do two things at once, viz.[2] remove the old senate and elect[3] a new one. I will order the senators to be summoned individually; I will consult[4] you concerning their lives; what you shall determine[5] about each shall be done.[6] But before a guilty man is punished, you shall elect as senator in[7] his place a brave and active[8] citizen." After that he sat down, and when the names had been cast into an urn,[9] ordered the name which came out first by lot to be called, and the man himself to be brought from the Senate House.[10] When the name was heard, each one began[11] to cry out that he was bad and wicked and worthy[12] of punishment. Then Pacuvius said, "I see what[13] your opinion of this man is; choose, therefore, a good and upright senator instead[14] of this bad and wicked one." This they were unable to do, and consequently the men escaped.—xxiii. 3 *(continued)*.

---

[1] Use here the gerundive.

[2] *Ut* is often used in an explanatory sentence.

[3] *Coopto.* Properly of election into a body by members of that body. Cf. our word *cooptative*.

[4] Remember the difference between *consulo te* and *tibi;* similarly between *metuo te* and *tibi*.

[5] *Censeo.*   [6] Recollect there is no *facior; fio* is the passive.

[7] The Latins would say, into his place.   [8] *Strenuus.*

[9] *Urna.* Cf. *Omne capax movet urna nomen.*   [10] *Curia.*

[11] The Latins are fond of using the infinitive in a case of this sort. It is called the Historic Infinitive.

[12] *Dignus.* Ablative with a noun ; *qui*, with subjunctive, with a verb, e.g. *puer dignus est qui ametur.*

[13] This is a dependent sentence.   [14] *Pro.*

LVI. *CICERO.*

I when[1] a youth loved Q. Maximus, the man who retook Tarentum, when[1] an old man, as if he had been of my[2] own age. For there was in that hero dignity tempered[3] by courtesy, nor had old age changed his character.[4] And[5] yet when I began to reverence him he was not very old, but yet already advanced[6] in life. For he had been consul for[7] the first time the year after I was born, and with him in his fourth consulship I set out when[1] a mere[8] youth as a soldier to Capua, and five years afterwards to Tarentum. Nor, indeed, was he more distinguished in arms than in civil[9] life. In his second consulship, when his colleague Carvilius remained[10] passive, he opposed to the utmost of his power Flaminius, the tribune of the people, when he proposed to divide the Gallic territory contrary to the wish of the Senate, and though[11] he was augur he had the boldness to say that those things were done under the best auspices which[12] were done for the good of the State.— *De Senectute,* 10.

---

[1] "When" in this sense is not expressed in Latin.

[2] *Æqualis.*　　　　　[3] *Condio.*　　　　　[4] *Mores.*

[5] *Quanquam.*　　　　　[6] *Ætate provectus.*

[7] Cf. *primum consul, iterum consul,* etc.

[8] A diminutive of *adolescens* will express this.

[9] *Toga.* Cf. *cedant arma togæ.*　　　　　[10] *Quiesco.*

[11] *Quum* must be followed by subjunctive when used in this sense. So *licet* and *quamvis; quanquam* and *etsi* take indicative.

[12] Recollect this is oblique narration.

LVII. *CÆSAR.*

Put into Oratio obliqua.

Titurius said, "You will do it too late, when greater forces of the enemy, with[1] the addition of the Germans, have assembled, or when some[2] disaster has been sustained[3] in the nearest winter quarters. The opportunity for deliberation is short. I think that Cæsar has set out for Italy; neither otherwise would the Carnutes have formed[4] the plan of killing[5] Tasgetius, nor would the Eburones, if he were at hand, come to the camp with such a great contempt for[6] us. I do not look to the enemy for advice, but to the fact itself. The Rhine is[7] at hand; the death of Ariovistus and our former victories are a[8] great annoyance to the Germans; Gaul is[9] exasperated at being reduced under the sway of the Roman people after receiving so many insults."[10]—*Bell. Gall.* v. 29.

[1] Abl. abs.

[2] *Aliquid calamitatis.* The Latins are fond of the genitive case after *aliquid.* Cf. *aliquid novi.*

[3] *Accipio.*

[4] *Inire consilium.*

[5] Use gerundive agreeing with substantive. This is really passive, though translated actively.

[6] Say "of us," and use *nostri,* because it means of us *collectively. Nostrum* means of us *individually.*

[7] *Subesse.*

[8] The Latins say *for* a great annoyance (*dolor*).

[9] *Ardeo* (neuter).

[10] *Contumelia.*

LVIII. *NEPOS.*

Fired with [1] annoyance at this, he formed plans to do away with the kings of the Lacedæmonians. But he perceived that he could not do that without the aid of the gods, because the Lacedæmonians were accustomed to refer everything to oracles. First of all he tried to corrupt the Delphic (oracle). Failing [2] in that, he tried Dodona. Being repulsed also from here, he said that he had undertaken vows which he must pay to Jupiter Hammon, thinking that he would more easily corrupt the Africans. When he had gone to Africa with this expectation, the priests of Jupiter greatly disappointed [3] him. For not only were they proof [4] against corruption, but even sent ambassadors to Lacedæmon to [5] accuse Lysander of [6] having attempted to corrupt the priests of the shrine. After being accused on this charge and acquitted by the [7] votes of the judges, he was killed by the Thebans.—*Lysander,* 3.

[1] Say, with this annoyance (*dolor*).

[2] *Cum id non potuisset.*

[3] *Fallo.* This verb sometimes means to escape the notice of. Cf. also *fidem fallere.*

[4] Literally *not able to be corrupted.*

[5] *Qui* with subjunctive or *ad* with the gerundive.

[6] Begin a sentence with *quod.* Cf. *Socrates damnatus est quod juventutem corrumperet.*

[7] *Sententia.*

LIX. *CÆSAR.*

About midnight Cæsar, using as guides the same men who had come as messengers from Iccius, sends archers[1] and slingers[2] to help[3] the townspeople. On their arrival a desire of fighting, together with the hope of defence, increased[4] for the Remi, while from the enemy for the same reason the hope of taking[5] the town departed. Accordingly, having lingered a short time about the town, and having laid waste the territory of the Remi, after[6] burning all the villages and buildings they could get[7] at, they hastened with all their forces to Cæsar's camp, and pitched their camp two miles off. This[8] camp, as was shown by the smoke and fires, extended in breadth more than eight miles.—*Bell. Gall.* ii. 6.

[1] *Sagittarius.*

[2] *Funditor.*

[3] *Subsidium.* Use *dativus propositi.*

[4] *Accedo.*

[5] Use the gerundive agreeing with the substantive, and recollect though translated actively it is really passive, e.g. *eo ad capiendam urbem,* I go for the city to be taken.

[6] Use abl. abs.

[7] *Adeo.*

[8] *Qui.* The Latins like to begin with a relative.

LX. *NEPOS.*

But Dion, relying [1] not so much on his forces as on their hatred [2] for the tyrant, with the greatest courage having set out with two merchant-ships [3] to attack a government fifty years old, protected by 500 ships of war, 10,000 cavalry, and 100,000 infantry, a thing which appeared marvellous to all nations, so easily overthrew [4] it, that three days after he had reached Sicily he entered Syracuse. From this it may be understood that no government is safe unless protected by the goodwill of the citizens. At that time Dionysius was away, and was waiting [5] in Italy for the fleet of his opponents, thinking that no one would come against him without great forces. This deceived him, for Dion, with those very forces which had been in the power of his opponent, crushed the pride [6] of the despotic party, and gained [7] possession of the whole of that part of Sicily.—*Dion,* 5.

---

[1] *Fretus* followed by ablative.

[2] *Odium Tyranni.* This may mean, according to the context, the hatred felt by or towards the tyrant. In the first case it is the subjective, in the second the objective genitive.

[3] *Navis oneraria.* A ship of war is *navis longa,* a transport *navis vectoria.*

[4] *Percello.*

[5] *Opperior* or *expecto.*

[6] *Regii spiritus.*

[7] *Potior.* Construction, gen. or abl., except in the expression *potiri rerum,* to be master of the world.

LXI. *SALLUST.*

I, O Jugurtha, received you into my kingdom when [1] small, having [2] lost your father, without hope, without resources, thinking that owing to my kindnesses I should be no less dear to you than if I had begotten [3] you; nor [4] was I mistaken in that. For to pass over other great and glorious [5] exploits of yours, very [6] lately returning from Numantia you covered [7] me and my kingdom with glory, [7] and by your valour made the Romans most friendly to us. Lastly, a thing which is most difficult among men, you have conquered envy by your fame. Now, since nature is bringing me the end of life, by this right hand, by my [8] royal honour I warn and beseech you to [9] hold dear those who are kinsmen to you by birth and brothers by my kindness, and not to prefer to attach to you strangers, [10] rather than to keep those joined to you by ties of blood.—*Jugurtha,* 10.

[1] Never translate this *when* in Latin. Cf. *puer hoc feci,* when a boy I did this.
[2] Ablative abs.
[3] *Gigno.*
[4] *Nec ea res me fefellit.*
[5] *Egregius (e grex).*
[6] *Novissime.*
[7] *Honorare gloriâ.*
[8] *Per regni fidem.*
[9] After a verb of beseeching translate to by *ut,* not to by *ne.*
[10] *Alieni.*

LXII. *CICERO.*

Antony led out two legions, the second and the thirty-
fifth, and two Prætorian regiments, one his own, the
other that of Silanus and part of the veterans.[1] He
marched[2] to meet us, because he thought that we only
had four legions of recruits.[3] But, in[4] order that we
might more safely reach the camp, Hirtius had sent us
by night the Martial legion, which I was accustomed to
command,[5] and two Prætorian regiments. When the
cavalry of Antony appeared, neither the Martial legion
nor the Prætorian regiments could be kept back. We
began to follow them under[6] compulsion, since we could
not restrain them. Antony kept[7] his forces in hand at a
neighbouring village, nor did he wish it to be known that
he had legions. He only displayed his cavalry and light-
armed[8] troops.—*Ep. ad Div.* x. 30.

---

[1] *Evocati*, i.e. those who had been discharged, but were liable to
be called out. Cf. our reserve men.
[2] *Obviam ire* or *venire alicui.*
[3] *Tiro.*
[4] When there is a comparative use *quo* instead of *ut.*
[5] *Præsum.* What does *præficio* mean ?
[6] *Coactus.*
[7] *Continere.*
[8] *Levis armatura.*

LXIII. *CÆSAR.*

Now when[1] the attention of all was occupied, Dumnorix begins to depart home from the camp with the cavalry of the Ædui, unknown[2] to Cæsar. On this being reported, Cæsar, having stopped his march and put[3] everything else in[3] the background, sends a great part of the cavalry to[4] pursue him, and orders him to be brought back. If he resisted and did not obey, he orders that he should be killed, thinking that he would do nothing as a prudent[5] man in his (Cæsar's) absence, since[6] he had disregarded his command when present. He, when summoned back, began[7] to resist, to defend himself by force, and to ask the aid of his followers, often crying out that he was free and of a free state. They, as[8] they were commanded, surround and kill the man.— *Bell. Gall.* v. 7.

[1] Use abl. abs. *animis impeditis.*
[2] *Cæsare insciente.*
[3] *Postpono.*
[4] *Ad* with gerundive.
[5] *Sanus.*
[6] Use *qui* causal with subj.
[7] Either use *cœpi* or the infinitive without *cœpi*, which will be historical.
[8] Use the verb impersonally.

LXIV. *LIVY.*

When Cneius Lentulus, a tribune of the soldiers, passing by on his horse saw the Consul, covered with gore, sitting on a rock, "Æmilius," says he, "whom alone the gods ought to regard as guiltless[1] of fault as regards this[2] day's disaster, take this horse while you have some[3] strength remaining. Do[4] not make this battle disastrous[5] by the death of a consul; even now without this there are tears and sorrow enough."[6] To this the Consul (replied), "O Cneius Cornelius, go[7] on in your valour; but beware[8] lest by delaying in vain you waste the short time you have to[9] escape from the hands of the enemy; go, tell the Senate publicly to[10] fortify the city of Rome and to strengthen it with garrisons before the victorious enemy arrives; privately tell Q. Fabius that Æmilius has lived and dies mindful of his advice."[11] —xxii. 49.

[1] *Insons.*

[2] *Hodierna clades.*

[3] Use *aliquid* with the genitive.

[4] *Ne feceris* or *noli facere.*

[5] *Funestus.*

[6] Use *satis* with the genitive.

[7] *Macte (magis aucte) virtute esto.*

[8] *Cave ne,* or omit the *ne.* The verb of course will be in the subjunctive.

[9] Lit. "of escaping."

[10] Use the jussive subjunctive. In oratio directa it would be "fortify the city."

[11] *Præcepta.*

LXV. *CÆSAR.*

On the next day, according to his custom, Cæsar led out his forces from both camps, and having advanced a short distance from the larger one, drew[1] up his army in battle array, and gave the enemy the opportunity of fighting. When he perceived that not[2] even then they came[3] forth, about midday he led back his army to the camp. Then at length Ariovistus sent a part of his forces to[4] attack the smaller camp. They fought like[5] lions on both sides till evening. At sunset Ariovistus led back his forces to the camp after[6] inflicting and receiving many wounds. When Cæsar inquired of the prisoners why[7] Ariovistus did not fight it out, he found this reason, because[8] the women used to declare from lots and auguries[9] whether[10] it was advantageous for war to be engaged in or not, and that they said as follows, " that it was not the will of heaven[11] that the Germans should conquer if they engaged in battle before the new moon."
—*Bell. Gall.* i. 50.

---

[1] *Aciem instruere.*
[2] *Ne—quidem,* meaning "not even" must have a word between.
[3] *Prodeo.*   [4] *Qui* with subj.   [5] *Acerrime.*
[6] Abl. abs.   Use *inferre* for "to inflict."
[7] Dependent sentence.
[8] *Quod.*   Subj., because it states what they said.
[9] *Vaticinatio.*
[10] In dependent sentences use *utrum—an, num—an, ne—an, —ne, —an.*
[11] *Fas.*   Opposed to *jus,* the laws of men.

F

LXVI. *NEPOS*.

When Tissaphernes, who at that time had the chief authority among the royal satraps,[1] learnt this, he asked for a truce,[2] pretending[3] that he was doing[4] his best to cause[5] an agreement between the king and the Lacedæmonian, but in reality to get forces, and he obtained it for[6] three months.   Each[7] party, moreover, swore that he would observe the truce without treachery. Agesilaus remained steadfast to this agreement in the most scrupulous way.[8]   On the other hand, Tissaphernes did nothing else but prepare for war.   Although the Lacedæmonian was aware of this, he yet kept his oath, and used[9] to say that by doing so he gained much, since[10] Tissaphernes by his perjury both alienated men from his[11] cause and made the gods angry against him, but that he by[12] respecting religious scruples gave confidence to his army.—*Agesilaus,* II.

[1] *Præfectus.*
[2] *Indutiæ.*
[3] *Simulo.*   Cf *quod non est simulo, dissimuloque quod est.*
[4] *Operam dare ut.*
[5] Use *convenire.*
[6] *Trimestris.*
[7] *Uterque.   Uter =* which of two.
[8] *Summâ fide.*
[9] " Used to " may often be translated by the imperfect.
[10] *Quod.*   Use subjunctive after it, because it is oblique narration.
[11] *Suæ res.   Res* must always be translated according to the context.
[12] *Religione conservatâ.*   Do not translate religion by *religio,* but by *pietas* or *cultus deorum.*

LXVII. CÆSAR.

Ariovistus made but a few replies to the demands[1] of Cæsar, but said a good deal about his own merits; that he had crossed the Rhine, not of his own accord, but being asked and summoned[2] by the Gauls; that he had left home and his relations not without great hope and great rewards; that he had settlements in Gaul granted by the Gauls themselves; that hostages had been given with their consent[3]; that he received by right of war the tribute[4] which the conquerors were wont[5] to lay on the conquered; that he had not made[6] war on the Gauls, but the Gauls on him; that all the states of Gaul had come to attack him, and had pitched their camps against him; that all those forces had been routed and overthrown by him in one battle; if they wished to try again,[7] that he was ready again to fight it out[8]; if they wished to enjoy peace, that it was unfair[9] to refuse to pay the tribute which they had voluntarily paid up to that time.— *Bell. Gall.* i. 44.

[1] *Postulatum.*
[2] *Arcesso.*
[3] *Voluntas.*
[4] *Stipendium.*
[5] All verbs in the subordinate sentence in oratio obliqua are in the subjunctive, because they do not state a fact.
[6] *Inferre bellum alicui.*
[7] When again means a second time use *iterum.*
[8] *Decertare. De* gives intensive force to a verb.
[9] *Iniquus.*

LXVIII. *LIVY.*

This was the first battle with Hannibal, by which it[1] was quite clear that the Carthaginian[2] was superior in cavalry, and that on that account the open plains such as lie between the Po[3] and the Alps were unsuited to the Romans for[4] waging war. Consequently, on the next night, after[5] the soldiers had been ordered to pack[6] up their baggage in silence, the camp was moved from the Ticinus, and they[7] hastened to the Po in order that if the[8] bridge of boats were not yet broken,[9] he might lead his forces across without confusion[10] and pursuit by the enemy. They reached Placentia before[11] Hannibal knew that they had set out from the Ticinus.—xxi. 47.

[1] *Facile apparuit* followed by acc. and infinitive.

[2] *Pœnus.*

[3] *Padus.*

[4] Use the gerundive.

[5] Use abl. abs.

[6] *Vasa colligere.*

[7] *Festino* or *propero.* Use verb impersonally.

[8] *Rates quibus junxerat flumen.* The Latins say *pontem facere in flumine.* We say *over.*

[9] *Resolvo.*

[10] *Tumultus.* This word is also used of a rising in Gaul.

[11] *Priusquam.* This word is usually separated, *prius* being put in the first sentence and *quam* in the next. It is followed by subjunctive or indicative. The former when purpose is implied, as here.

LXIX. *CICERO.*

I can dilate[1] upon very many delights of country[2] life, but I feel that what I have said has been too long. You will pardon[3] me, however, for I have been carried away by my zeal for country life, and old age is naturally[4] rather garrulous,[5] that[6] I may not[6] seem to defend it from all faults. Therefore Curius, after he had triumphed[7] over the Samnites, the Sabines, and Pyrrhus, spent his last years in this life. When the Samnites brought to Curius sitting by his hearth a great weight of gold, they were rejected ; for he said that he did not consider it a fine thing to have gold, but to command those who[3] had it.— *De Senectute,* 55.

[1] *Persequor* with acc.
[2] *Res rusticæ.* Cf. *res adversæ, res secundæ.*
[3] *Ignosco* or *veniam dare,* both with dat.
[4] Lit. " by nature."
[5] *Loquax.* Rather may often be expressed by a comparative.
[6] That not when a purpose is *ne,* when a consequence *ut non.* Similarly *ne quis, ne quid, ut nemo, ut nihil.*
[7] *Triumphare de.*
[3] Recollect this is oblique narration.

LXX. *SALLUST.*

I [1] hold it as a thing well ascertained that words do not give [2] additional valour, and that an army does not become energetic [3] instead [4] of slothful, [5] or brave instead [4] of frightened, by the speech of its commander. So [6] much boldness is wont to be displayed in war as [6] by nature or character [7] is in the disposition of each. You would exhort to no purpose one who is [8] aroused neither by fame nor dangers. Fear stops [9] their ears. But I have summoned you to [10] give you a little advice, at the same time to [10] disclose to you the reason of my plan. You know, indeed, soldiers, what [11] disaster the sloth and cowardice of Lentulus brought upon himself and us, and how, while I [12] wait for forces from the city, I [13] was unable to set out into Gaul.—*Catiline*, 58.

[1] *Compertum habeo.*   Cf. also *mihi persuasum habeo.*
[2] Lit. add valour.
[3] *Strenuus.*
[4] *Pro.*
[5] *Ignavus.*
[6] *Tantus—quantus.*   Cf. *talis—qualis, tot—quot.*   These are called correlatives.
[7] *Mores.*
[8] Turn the passive into active.
[9] *Officio.*
[10] Use *ut.*
[11] Dependent sentence.
[12] *Opperior* or *expecto.*
[13] *Nequeo.*

LXXI. *CÆSAR.*

While[1] these things were being done by Cæsar, the Treviri having[2] collected great forces of infantry and cavalry were preparing to attack Labienus and the one legion that was wintering[3] in their territory, and already they were distant from him not more than a two days' march, when[4] they learn that two legions sent by Cæsar had arrived. Having[2] pitched their camp five miles away, they determine to wait for the forces of the Germans. Labienus, on[2] hearing the enemy's design, hoping that owing[5] to their rashness[6] there would be some opportunity of fighting, having left five regiments to[7] guard the baggage, sets out with twenty-five regiments and a great force of cavalry against the enemy. There was between Labienus and the enemy a river difficult[8] to cross and with precipitous[9] banks. He neither intended[10] to cross this himself, nor did he think that the enemy would cross it. He says openly at the council, "since[11] the forces of the Germans are said to be approaching, I will not hazard[12] my fortune and that of the army, but will strike my camp at daybreak."—*Bell. Gall.* vi. 7.

[1] *Dum*, while, has a preference for the present tense.
[2] Abl. abs.   [3] *Hiemare.*
[4] *Quum* when merely temporal is followed by the indicative.
[5] Ablative of cause.   [6] *Temeritas.*
[7] Use predicative dative of *præsidium.*
[8] Lit. "of difficult crossing" (*transitus*).
[9] *Præruptus.*   [10] *In animo habere.* Cf. *mihi est in animo.*
[11] Put to the end into oblique narration.
[12] *Devocare in dubium.*

LXXII. *NEPOS.*

He did not, however, escape the envy [1] of his (fellow) citizens.   For, owing to the same fear in consequence of which Miltiades was condemned, he was ostracized,[2] and withdrew to Argos to [3] live.   While living there in great honour owing to his great merits, the Lacedæmonians sent ambassadors to Athens to [4] accuse him in [5] his absence of[6] having formed an alliance with the king to overthrow Greece.   On this charge he was convicted of treason [7] in [5] his absence.   When he heard it, because he did not think he was safe enough at Argos, he changed [8] his abode to Corcyra.—*Themistocles*, 8.

[1] *Invidia.*   It often means " unpopularity."

[2] *Testularum suffragiis ejectus.*   Lit. banished by the votes of the tiles.   Look out the word ostracize.

[3] *Habito.*   Use the supine in *um*, which is used after verbs of motion.

[4] Use *qui* with subj.

[5] Use the adjective *absens* agreeing with him.

[6] *Quod.*   With subj., because it is what they said.   Cf. *Socrates damnatus est quod juventutem corrumperet.*

[7] *Proditio.*   Treason may often be translated by *læsa majestas.*

[8] *Demigrare.*

LXXIII. *CÆSAR.*

Consequently, when[1] the winter was not yet over, having[1] collected the four nearest legions, he unexpectly[2] marches into the territory of the Nervii, and before[3] they could either assemble or escape, having[1] captured a great quantity of cattle and men, and having[1] handed[4] over this booty to the soldiers, compelled them to[5] capitulate and give him hostages. Having quickly finished this business, he led his legions back again into winter[6] quarters. Having called a council of Gaul in the early spring, as he was accustomed to do, when the others came, with[7] the exception of the Senones, Carnutes, and Treviri, thinking that this was the beginning of war and revolt,[8] he transfers the council to Paris.[9]— *Bell. Gall.* vi. 3.

[1] Abl. abs.

[2] *De improviso.* Cf. also *de industriâ, e vestigio,* etc.

[3] *Priusquam,* followed by subj. and indic., by the latter when it is merely temporal.

[4] *Concedo.*

[5] *In deditionem venire.*

[6] *Hiberna.* Understand *castra.* Cf. *æstiva.*

[7] *Præter.*

[8] *Defectio.*

[9] *Lutetia.*

LXXIV. *LIVY.*

The Roman ambassadors, as it had been commanded them at Rome, crossed[1] over from Carthage into Spain, to visit the states, to allure[2] them to an alliance, or to turn them away from the Carthaginians. They first came to the Bargusii, and being kindly received by them because they were disgusted[3] with the Carthaginian rule, they roused[4] many nations across the Ebro[5] to a desire for a new[6] state of things. From thence they[7] came to the Volciani, whose answer famous[8] throughout Spain turned away the other nations from the Roman alliance.[9] For thus the eldest man among them replied at the council: " Are you not ashamed,[10] Romans, to demand that we should prefer your friendship to that of the Carthaginians, seeing[11] that though allies you have abandoned the Saguntines, who have done so, more cruelly than the Cathaginians have done? I[12] give it as my opinion that you should seek for allies there where the disaster of[13] Saguntum is unknown."—xxi. 19.

[1] *Trajicio.* This verb is both transitive and intransitive.

[2] *Pellicio.*

[3] *Tædet*, with accusative of person and genitive of thing, or infinitive. Similarly *piget, pudet, pænitet, miseret.*

[4] *Erigo.*   [5] *Hiberus.*   [6] *Nova fortuna.*

[7] The Latins are fond of using a verb impersonally, e.g. *pugnatum est quinque horas.*

[8] *Celeber.* This word generally means " populous."

[9] *Societas.* Cf. *societatem inire cum aliquo.*

[10] *Quæ verecundia est* followed by acc. or infin.

[11] *Quum.*   [12] *Censeo* is used of giving an official opinion.

[13] Use an adjective. Cf. *pugna Cannensis*, the battle of Cannæ.

LXXV. *SALLUST.*

All bad precedents[1] have sprung from good ones ; but when the power comes to those who are ignorant or less good, that new precedent is transferred from those who were deserving and fit persons (for punishment) to those who are not deserving and not fit. The Lacedæmonians after[2] the defeat of the Athenians set over them thirty men to[3] manage[4] their state. They at first began[5] to put to death without[6] trial all[7] the worse men and those hated by all. The people were pleased[5] at this, and said it was done according[3] to their deserts. Afterwards they killed[5] at[9] their pleasure good and bad alike.[10] Thus the state oppressed with slavery paid[11] the bitter penalty of its foolish joy.—*Catiline*, li. 27.

[1] *Exemplum.*

[2] Either *quum* with pluperfect subj., or ablative absolute.

[3] *Qui* with subjunctive. Remember you cannot use infinitive of the purpose in Latin.

[4] *Tractare.*

[5] Use historical infinitives.

[6] *Indemnatus* or *causâ indictâ.*

[7] Use the superlative of the adjective with *quisque.* Cf. *Fortissimus quisque interfectus est.*

[8] *Merito.*   [9] *Lubidinose.*   [10] *Juxta.*   [11] *Dare pœnam.*

LXXVI. *CÆSAR.*

On learning these[1] things the chiefs of Britain, who after the battle was over had assembled to do those things which Cæsar had ordered, conferred[2] together, and since they were aware that cavalry, ships, and corn were wanting to the Romans, and were acquainted with the small number of soldiers owing to the smallness[3] of the camp, which was even smaller on this account because Cæsar had brought his legions without heavy[4] baggage, they thought the best thing to do was to[5] make a rebellion, to cut off our men from supplies,[6] and to prolong matters till winter, because if they were conquered and stopped from returning, they thought that no one afterwards would cross over into Britain for the purpose of making[7] war.—*Bell. Gall.* iv. 30.

[1] Say " which." The Latins like to begin with a relative.
[2] *Inter se colloqui.*
[3] *Exiguitas.*
[4] *Impedimenta* (plural). The light baggage of the soldier was *sarcina.*
[5] Put this in abl. abs.
[6] *Commeatus.* It also means "furlough."
[7] *Bellum inferre.* To act on the defensive is *bellum defendere.*

LXXVII. *LIVY.*

While the elephants were taken[1] across Hannibal had sent 500 Numidian cavalry to the Roman camp to[2] reconnoitre the whereabouts[3] and number of their forces, and what they were preparing (to do). The 300 cavalry sent, as we have before said, from the mouth of the Rhone, meet[4] this squadron of cavalry. A battle, fiercer than[5] in proportion to the number of the combatants, takes place; for, besides many wounds, the slaughter also on both sides was nearly equal, and the rout and panic of the Numidians gave the victory to the Romans already wearied[6] out. Of[7] the victors as many as 160 fell, and not all Romans, but some Gauls; of the vanquished, more than 200.—xxi. 29.

[1] *Trajicio.*

[2] *Speculatum.* The supine in *um* can be used after a verb of motion. Cf. *spectatum veniunt, veniunt spectentur ut ipsæ.*

[3] Lit. where, how great, and what. This is, of course, a dependent sentence.

[4] *Occurro* followed by dative. So *obviam ire alicui.*

[5] *Quam pro numero.*

[6] *Admodum fessi.*

[7] Lit. he conquered as many as, etc.

LXXVIII. *CÆSAR.*

Cæsar, after delaying[1] a few days in their territory,[2] having[3] burnt all the villages and buildings and cut[4] down the corn, betook[5] himself into the territory of the Ubii, and having promised[6] them his help if they were hard pressed by the Suevi, learnt the following facts from them : that the Suevi, as soon as they had found out by scouts[7] that a bridge was being made, having held a council according to their custom, had despatched messengers in all directions (ordering) that people should leave the towns and place their families[8] and all their property in the woods, and that all who could bear arms should assemble at one place; that this was chosen as being almost the centre of those regions which the Suevi possessed[9]; that here they had determined to await the approach of the Romans and to fight[10] a pitched battle. —*Bell. Gall.* iv. 19.

[1] *Moror.* This verb is sometimes used in another sense, e.g. *Nil moror hæc,* I care nothing for this.

[2] *Fines.* In the singular it means "end."

[3] Abl. abs., or *quum* with pluperfect subj.

[4] *Succido.*

[5] *Se recipere.*

[6] *Polliceor.* Generally used of promising spontaneously. Cf. *Ultro polliceor, promitto sæpe rogatus.*

[7] *Explorator.*

[8] Say "wife and children." *Familia* means household.

[9] This being a subordinate clause in oratio obliqua, the subj. must be used.

[10] *Decertare.* *De* as a prefix gives intensive force.

LXXIX. *CICERO.*

What state was there ever before, I do not say of the Athenians, which is said to have been formerly mistress[1] of the Sea to[2] a considerable extent, nor of the Carthaginians, who were very powerful in their fleet and maritime affairs, nor of the Rhodians, whose naval discipline and fame has remained even[3] to our age—what state, I say, was ever so insignificant, what island so small, as[4] not to be able of itself to defend its harbours and territory and some part of the country and coast bordering on the sea? But, by[5] heaven! for[6] some successive[7] years before the Gabinian law the great Roman people, whose name has remained even[3] to our days invincible in naval battles, were deprived[5] of a great, aye,[9] the greatest part, not only of what[10] was useful to them, but of their honour and dominion.—*Pro Lege Manilia*, 18.

[1] *Tenere mare.*

[2] *Satis late.*

[3] *Usque ad nostram memoriam.*

[4] Use *qui* with subjunctive, and cf. *nemo erat quin (qui non) fleret.* In these cases *qui* = such as.

[5] *Hercle* (lit. by Hercules), *Pol* (by Pollux), *Ecastor* (by Castor), are all Latin oaths.

[6] Duration of time.

[7] *Continuus.*

[8] *Careo.* Cf. *Carmina sola carent fato mortemque repellunt.*

[9] *Ac.*

[10] *Utilitas.*

LXXX. *CÆSAR.*

Ambiorix, elated [1] by this victory, immediately sets out with his cavalry for the Aduatuci, who were neighbouring to his kingdom. He stops [2] neither night nor day, and orders the infantry to follow after him. Having told them what had happened and roused [3] the Aduatuci, on the following day he comes to the Nervii and exhorts them not to let [4] slip the opportunity [5] of freeing themselves for ever, and avenging [6] themselves on the Romans for those wrongs they have received. He points out that two staff-officers [7] had been killed, and a great part of the army destroyed; that there was no [8] difficulty in the legion that was wintering with Cicero being suddenly surprised [9] and destroyed. He promises his assistance to this end, and easily persuades the Nervii by this speech.—*Bell. Gall.* v. 38.

[1] *Sublatus.*

[2] *Intermitto.*

[3] *Concitare.*

[4] *Dimitto.*

[5] *Occasio.*

[6] Cf. *Ulcisci aliquem.* .

[7] *Legati.*

[8] *Nihil est negotii.*

[9] *Opprimo.*

(LXXXI.) *SALLUST.*

When this was known at Rome, the Senate declares
Catiline and Manlius enemies;[1] and fixes a day for the
rest before which they would be allowed[2] with[3] impunity
to lay down their arms. Furthermore, it passes a decree
that the consuls should hold[4] a levy, that Antony should
hasten with an army to pursue Catiline, and that Cicero
should[5] protect the city. At this time the Empire of the
Roman people appeared to me by far in its most pitiable
light ; for, though[6] everything subdued by arms obeyed[7]
it from the East to the West, though at home there was
abundance[8] of ease and wealth, which things mortals
consider the chief blessings, still there[9] were citizens who
were ready[10] to ruin themselves and the state with
stubborn determination. For, though there were two
decrees of the Senate, no one out of such a great number
had either induced by reward disclosed[11] the conspiracy
or left the camp of Catiline — *Catiline, 3§.*

---

[1] *Hostis. Inimicus* means a private foe.

[2] *Licet,* always used impersonally with dative. Cf. *Nobis licet esse beatis.*

[3] *Sine fraude.*   [4] *Dilectum habere.*

[5] Use a double dative. Cf. *Exitio est avidum mare nautis.*

[6] Though may be translated by *quum, licet, quamvis, quanquam, etsi ;* the first three with subjunctive, the last two with indicative.

[7] *Pareo* (lit. to appear for, and therefore followed by dative).

[8] *Adfluere.*

[9] *Sunt qui* and *inveniuntur qui* are followed by subjunctive, because *qui* in this case means " such as."

[10] *Perditum ire.* ·   [11] *Patefacio.*

G

LXXXII. *LIVY.*

There during[1] the greater part of the winter he kept under[2] cover his army, often and for a long time inured[3] to all human ills, but inexperienced in and unaccustomed to prosperity. Consequently[4] those whom no amount of ill had conquered were ruined by excessive[5] prosperity and immoderate pleasure, and the more[6] in proportion as, owing to their novelty, they had plunged more[6] eagerly into them. For sleep and wine and banquets so enervated their bodies and spirits that hereafter their past victories protected them more than their present power, and this was considered among those versed[7] in military affairs a greater mistake of their leader than the[8] fact that he had not immediately after the battle[9] of Cannæ led them to Rome. For that delay[10] seemed only to have deferred[11] victory, but this mistake to have taken[12] away their strength to[13] conquer.—xxiii. 18.

[1] Time *when* is put in the ablative, *how long* in the accusative.

[2] *In tectis.*   [3] Lit. hardened (*duratus*) against.

[4] Turn this passive into an active sentence.

[5] *Nimius.*

[6] *Quo—eo.* Cf. *quo melior eo beatior*, the better you are the happier you are.

[7] *Peritus* and *imperitus* take a genitive.

[8] *Quod.*   [9] *Pugna Cannensis.*

[10] *Cunctatio.* Who was called *cunctator?* Cf. *Unus homo nobis cunctando restituit rem.*

[11] *Differo.*   [12] *Adimo.*

[12] Not infinitive, but *ad vincendum.*

LXXXIII. *NEPOS.*

This deed filled [1] all with the greatest dismay; for no one, now that man was killed, thought himself safe. He, however, having [2] removed his opponent, more freely divided among the soldiers the goods of those whom he knew had been opposed [3] to him. When these had been distributed, since his daily expenses were becoming very great, his money quickly began [4] to fail, nor did he know where to put his hands save [5] on the property of his friends. This action was of such a kind, [6] that while he gained [7] the favour of the soldiers he lost the nobles. He was overcome with anxiety at this, and, being unaccustomed to be evil spoken of, [8] he was annoyed [9] at being in [10] bad odour with those by whose praises a little before he had been extolled to heaven. —*Dion*, 7.

[1] Cf. *injicere timorem alicui.*
[2] Either ablative absolute, or *quum* with subjunctive.
[3] Cf. *adversus aliquem sentire.*
[4] *Cœpi.* Recollect that *cœptus sum* is used before a passive infinitive, e.g. *urbs cœpta est capi.*
[5] *Nisi.*
[6] *Ejusmodi ut.*
[7] *Reconcilio.*
[8] *Male audire.*
[9] *Ægre ferre, graviter ferre,* or *non animo æquo ferre.*
[10] *Male existimari ab aliquo.*

LXXXIV. *CÆSAR.*

Litavicus,[1] after receiving the army, when he was distant from Gergovia about thirty miles, having[1] suddenly called the soldiers together, says with tears, "Whither, soldiers, are we marching? all our cavalry, all our nobility have perished. The chiefs of the state, falsely[2] accused of treason, have been put to death unheard[3] by the Romans. Learn these facts from those who have escaped from the actual massacre[4]; for I, owing[1] to my brothers and all my relations being slain, am prevented[5] by my grief from telling you what took place." Those men whom he had instructed what[6] he wished said are brought forward, and tell the people the same[7] story Litavicus had done, viz., "that all the knights of the Ædui were killed because they were said to have conferred[8] with the Arverni; that they had hidden themselves among the throng[9] of soldiers and had escaped from the massacre." The Ædui raise a shout and beg Litavicus to look[10] after their interests.— *Bell. Gall.* vii. 38.

[1] Ablative absolute.   [2] *Insimulatus.*

[3] *Causâ indictâ.*   [4] *Cædes.*

[5] *Prohibeor* with infinitive, or *quominus* and the subjunctive.

[6] Observe the sentence is dependent.

[7] *Idem—qui.*   [8] *Colloquor.*   [9] *Multitudo.*

[10] *Consulo.* Mind the difference between *consulo te* and *consulo tibi*, and cf. *metuo te* and *metuo tibi*.

LXXXV. *CICERO.*

Now, although you see with [1] what rapidity these things were performed, yet they ought [2] not to be passed over by me in speaking. For who ever, either in his zeal for [3] transacting [4] business or acquiring [5] gain, was able in so short a time to visit so many places, to accomplish such great journeys as quickly, as under [6] the command of Pompey the fury of war sailed [7] on? For he, when [6] the sea was as yet unfit for [3] navigation, visited Sicily and explored Africa; from thence he came with his fleet to Sardinia, and strengthened there three granaries [9] of the state with the strongest garrisons and fleets. When he had withdrawn from thence into Italy, having [6] previously strengthened the two Spains and Cisalpine Gaul with garrisons and ships, and [6] having also sent ships to the coast of the Illyrian Sea, he furnished [10] the two seas of Italy with very great fleets and very strong garrisons.— *Pro Lege Manilia*, 12.

[1] Observe this is dependent.
[2] Use the gerundive.
[3] The Latins would use the genitive.
[4] *Obire negotium.*
[5] *Consequi quæstum.*
[6] Use abl. abs.
[7] *Navigo.*
[3] *Ad navigandum.*
[9] *Frumentaria subsidia.*
[10] *Adorno.*

LXXXVI. *SALLUST.*

Cæsar, when [1] his turn came, on being asked his opinion, spoke words of the following kind: "It behoves all men, O conscript fathers, who deliberate on [2] difficult matters, to be free [3] from hatred, friendship, anger, and pity. The mind, when those feelings are [4] in the way, does not easily foresee the truth, nor has any [5] man followed his passion [6] and his interest [7] at the same time. If you steadily [8] direct your understanding, it prevails; if passion possesses you, it holds [9] sway, and the understanding has no power. I can tell you, conscript fathers, what bad resolutions kings and nations have made under [10] the impulse of anger or pity, but I prefer to tell you those things which our ancestors did rightly and properly contrary to their passions. In the Macedonian war which we waged with King Perses, the state of the Rhodians, which had grown [11] by the help of the Roman people, was faithless and opposed to us; but when on [12] the conclusion of the war they [13] deliberated about the Rhodians, our ancestors let them go unpunished, lest any [14] one should say that the war was begun more for the sake of riches than of wrongs (received)."—*Catiline*, 51.

---

[1] "When it was come to him."   [2] *De dubiis rebus.*

[3] *Vacuus* with abl.   [4] *Officere.*

[5] When all are excluded use *quisquam* or *ullus*, when included *quivis* or *quilibet.*

[6] *Lubido.*   [7] *Usus.*   [8] *Intendo.*

[9] *Dominor.* Cf. *Infelix lolium et steriles dominantur avenæ.*

[10] Impelled by.   [11] *Cresco. Augeo* is to increase transitively.

[12] Use abl. abs.   [13] *Consulo.* Use it impersonally.

[14] After *num, si, nisi, ne,* translate any by *quis.*

LXXXVII. *LIVY.*

While[1] the Romans wasted[2] their time in sending[3] embassies, Hannibal, because he had a soldiery weary with battles and work, gave them a rest of a few days, having posted[4] pickets[5] to[6] guard the pent-houses[7] and other works. In the meantime he roused their feelings, at[8] one time by inspiring them with anger against the foe, at another time by hope of rewards; but when he declared before a meeting[9] that the plunder of the captured city should belong[10] to the soldiers, all were so excited that if the signal were at once given it[11] seemed that no power could resist them. The Saguntines, though[12] they had had rest from battle for several days, neither attacking nor attacked, yet[12] neither by night nor day had ever flagged[13] at the work, so that they built a new wall on that side where[14] the breach was made.—xxi. 11.

[1] Use *dum* with a present.   [2] *Terere tempus.*
[3] Use gerundive, which recollect, though translated actively, is really passive.
[4] *Dispono* is used of posting troops, etc.   [5] *Statio.*
[6] *Ad custodiam* or *dativus propositi.*
[7] *Vinea* or *testudo.* Look out meanings of latter word.
[8] *Nunc—nunc* or *alias—alias.*
[9] *Concio* is used for a meeting of the soldiers.
[10] Lit. should be of the soldiers.
[11] Lit. it seemed to be able to be resisted by no force.
[12] Though and yet may often be put into Latin by *ut—ita* with indicatives.
[13] *Cesso. Desino* means to cease.
[14] Lit. where it was opened with ruins.

LXXXVIII. *CÆSAR.*

Having[1] received the hostages, he leads back his army
to the sea, and finds the ships repaired.[2] Having
launched[3] these, because[4] he had a great number of
prisoners and several ships had been lost in a storm, he
determined to convey the army back by two embarka-
tions.[5] Now so it[6] happened, that out of such a great
number of ships, during so many voyages, neither in this
nor the former year any ship at all that[7] carried soldiers
was lost; but of those which were sent back to him
empty from the continent, the soldiers of the former
embarkation being landed, and those which Labienus
had superintended[8] the making of, very few reached
their destination.—*Bell. Gall.* v. 23.

[1] Either abl. abs. or *quum* with pluperfect subj.

[2] *Reficio.*

[3] *Deduco.* The opposite word is *subduco.*

[4] *Quod* here states a fact. It is therefore followed by indicative.

[5] *Commeatus.* This word has several meanings, viz. "supplies,"
"furlough."

[6] After *accidit* (it happened), *fit, sequitur, restat,* etc., translate
that by *ut.*

[7] *Qui* followed by subjunctive because it means "such as."

[8] *Curo.* This verb is followed by gerundive, e.g. *curabo pontem
faciendum.*

LXXXIX. *SALLUST.*

While[1] this was going on at Rome, Manlius sent some of his followers as ambassadors to Marcius Rex with a message of the following kind: "We[2] call gods and men to witness that we have taken up arms neither against our country[3] nor to cause danger to others, but that our persons may be safe from wrong. For we in wretchedness and poverty, owing[4] to the violence and cruelty of the usurers,[5] are most of us deprived[6] of our native land, all of us of our character[7] and fortune. Nor[8] has any one of us been allowed to take[9] advantage of the law after the custom of our ancestors, nor having lost his property to keep his person free; so great has been the severity[10] of the usurers and the prætor."— *Catiline*, 33.

---

[1] *Dum*, while, is usually followed by a present.

[2] *Testari.*

[3] Note the difference between *patria, rus, regio.*

[4] Use ablatives of cause.

[5] *Fenerator.*

[6] *Expers* (*ex pars*) with abl. or gen. Translate *any* after *expers* by *omnis.* Cf. *exsors*, which is a similar word.

[7] *Fama.*

[8] Nor has it been allowed (*licet* always impersonal) to any (all excluded).

[9] *Uti.*

[10] *Sævitia.*

XC. *CICERO.*

I will do the best I can, Lælius, for I have often heard the complaints of my contemporaries [1] (according to the old proverb, " birds [2] of a feather flock together ")— complaints which Salinator and Albinus, men of consular rank, used to utter, not [3] only because [4] they were without pleasures, without which they thought life not [5] worth living, but also because they were despised by those by whom they had been accustomed to be honoured. They did not appear to me to blame that which was deserving of blame. For if [6] this happened through the fault of old age, the same things would happen [7] to me and all other old men, the old age of many of whom I have known to be without complaint, since [8] they were not annoyed [9] at being freed from the trammels of the passions, and were not despised by their friends.—*De Senectute,* 7.

[1] *Æquales,* properly those of equal age.

[2] *Pares cum paribus facillime congregantur.*

[3] Not only—but also may often be rendered by *tum—tum* or *quum—tum.*

[4] *Quod* will have subjunctive here, because it is what they said. Cf. *Socrates accusatus est quod juventutem corrumperet.*

[5] Literally "nothing," *nullus.*

[6] Put this in imperfect subj., because it is implied it does not happen. Cf. *si quid haberem darem,* if I had anything (which I have not) I would give it.

[7] *Usu venire.*

[8] *Qui* followed by subjunctive or *qui* causal will express this.

[9] *Ægre* or *moleste ferre.*

XCI. *CÆSAR.*

Now on the first arrival of our army they made frequent [1] sallies [2] from the town, and engaged in slight skirmishes with our men; afterwards, having [3] fortified themselves with a rampart [4] of twelve feet, of fifteen miles in circumference, and with several forts, they kept themselves in the town. When, on the pent-houses [5] being moved [6] up and a mound raised, they saw a tower being erected at a distance, they first of all began [7] to jeer from the wall and to taunt them saying, " Why [8] is such a great engine being erected at such a distance? With what hands or what strength do you, especially since you are men of such insignificant [9] stature, expect to place a tower of such magnitude on the walls?"—*Bell. Gall.* ii. 30.

[1] *Creber. Frequens* means " crowded."

[2] *Excursio.*

[3] Use the passive participle of *communio* in a middle sense.

[4] *Vallum. Vallus* means the palisade.

[5] *Vinea.* Use abl. abs.

[6] *Ago.*

[7] " Began to " may often be translated by present infinitive. This is called the historical infinitive.

[8] Turn into *oratio obliqua.* Questions in the 2nd person are to be rendered in *oratio obliqua* by imp. or plup. subjunctive, questions in the 1st and 3rd by the acc. and infin., e.g.

Why are you advancing? (2nd) *cur progrederentur.*

Why did you sing? (2nd) *cur cecinissent.*

Why is the slave away? (3rd) *cur abesse servum.*

Why are we living there? (1st) *cur se ibi vivere.*

[9] *Tantulus.*

XCII. *NEPOS.*

Thrasybulus the son of Lycus was an Athenian. If merit[1] of itself without fortune is to be gauged,[2] I[3] almost think I should place him first of all men. The following is without doubt. I place no one before him in honour, consistency, magnanimity,[4] and love towards his country. For though many have wished, and yet few been able to free their country from one tyrant, it[5] fell to his lot to[6] free it from slavery when oppressed by thirty tyrants. But somehow[7] or other, though no one surpassed him in these qualities, many outstripped[8] him in reputation.[9] In the first place, in the Peloponnesian war he performed many achievements without Alcibiades, while Alcibiades did nothing without him; yet he (Alcibiades) by some innate[10] good fortune got[11] the credit for all these.—*Thrasybulus*, 1.   .

[1] *Virtus.* This word may be translated in many ways. "Manliness" is the most exact translation.

[2] *Pondero.*

[3] *Haud scio, nescio an* or *dubito an*, followed by subj.

[4] *Magnitudo animi* or *magnus animus.* Cf. adversity, *res adversa, res secundæ, ingratus animus.* There is no one Latin word for magnanimity, adversity, prosperity, ingratitude.

[5] *Huic contigit ut. Fit, restat, sequitur, accidit* are all followed by *ut.*

[6] *In libertatem vindicare.*

[7] *Nescio quomodo.* Similarly *nescio quid*, something or other.

[8] *Præcurro.*

[9] *Nobilitas.*

[10] *Naturalis.*

[11] *Lucri facio*, or as one word *lucrifacio.*

XCIII. *CÆSAR.*

Cæsar first of all sends Brutus, a youth,[1] with six regiments, afterwards Caius Fabius, his staff-officer, with seven others ; lastly in[2] person, since they were fighting more fiercely, he brings up fresh men as a[3] reinforcement. When the battle had been restored and the enemy driven back, he hastens thither where[4] he had sent Labienus ; he withdraws four regiments from the nearest redoubt ; he orders a part of the cavalry to follow him, part to go round the outside fortifications and to attack the enemy in[5] the rear. Labienus, when neither the ramparts nor the ditches were able to withstand the attack of the enemy, informs Cæsar by messengers what[6] he thinks ought to be done. Cæsar hastens up to[7] take part in the battle.—*Bell. Gall.* vii. 87.

---

[1] *Adolescens. Juvenis* means a man up to forty-five.

[2] " In person " may often be translated by *ipse.* Cf. *ipse vidi.*

[3] Use predicative dative of *subsidium.*

[4] *Quo,* because it means *to* which place. *Qua* means *in* which place.

[5] *A tergo.* Cf. *a latere, a fronte.*

[6] This sentence is dependent.

[7] *Interesse prælio.*

XCIV. *NEPOS.*

The Athenians long missed [1] him, not [2] only in war but also in peace. For he was a man of [3] such great generosity that, though he had estates [4] and gardens in several places, he never placed a guard over them for the purpose of preserving the produce, lest any [5] one should be prevented from [6] enjoying such things as each one wished. Footmen [7] always followed him with money, so that if any one needed [8] his assistance he might have something [9] to give him at once, lest by putting him off he should seem to refuse him. Often on [10] seeing some one whom he had met [11] by accident badly clothed, he gave him his cloak. Daily [12] he had such a dinner cooked that he invited all whom he happened [13] to see in the forum uninvited. His [14] protection, his assistance, his wealth were at the disposal of all. He enriched many. He buried at his own expense several poor men, since [15] they had not left enough to be buried with.—*Cimon*, 4.

[1] *Desidero.*　　　　[2] *Non solum—sed etiam*, or *quum—tum.*

[3] Ablative of quality.　　　[4] *Prædium.*

[5] After *num, si, nisi, ne*, translate any by *quis.*

[6] *Quominus* with subj. A common construction after verbs of preventing.

[7] *Pedissequus.*　　　　　　[8] *Indigeo* with genitive.

[9] What he might give.　　　[10] *Quum* with imperfect subj.

[11] *Fortuito offensus.*

[12] *Quotidie.* When there is increase or decrease, *indies.*

[13] This being indefinite is put in the subjunctive.

[14] Literally, There was wanting to no man his, etc.

[15] *Qui* with subjunctive. This is *qui* causal.

XCV. *NEPOS.*

Now Darius, having[1] returned from Europe to Asia, when[2] his friends urged him to reduce Greece under his sway, prepared a fleet of 500 ships, and put[3] in command of it Datis and Artaphernes, and gave them 200,000 infantry and 10,000 cavalry, alleging[4] as a reason, that he was an enemy to the Athenians, because[5] by their aid the Ionians had taken Sardis and slain his garrison. Those commanders of the king having[6] brought their fleet to land at Eubœa, quickly took Eretria and hurried[7] off to Asia, and sent[7] to the king all the citizens of that territory. After that they approached Attica, and led their forces to the plain of Marathon.—*Miltiades*, 4.

[1] Use *quum* with pluperfect subj.

[2] Abl. abs. Also use *hortor* with *ut.*

[3] *Præficio*, with acc. of person put in command and dat. of what he is put in command of.

[4] *Causam interserens.*

[5] *Quod.* As it does not here state a *fact*, it will be followed by subjunctive.

[6] *Appellere navem.* Use abl. abs.

[7] *Abripio.* The Latins put one verb in the passive participle. Cf. *pontem captum incendit*, he took and burned the bridge.

XCVI. *NEPOS.*

This joy was not very lasting [1] to Alcibiades. For when all honours [2] had been decreed to him, and the management of the whole state at [3] home and abroad placed [4] in his hand so that it should be carried on by his will alone, and he himself had demanded that [5] two colleagues should be given him, and [6] that was not refused, having set out with a fleet for Asia, because he was [7] unsuccessful there he fell into odium, [8] for they thought that there was nothing he could not do. The [9] result of this was that they blamed [10] him for all unsuccessful operations, since they said that he had either acted with negligence or malice. He was feared no less than he was loved, lest elated by his prosperity and great resources he should be desirous of sovereign [11] power. The result of this was that they took [12] away his command in his absence, and put another in his place. When he heard this he was unwilling to return home, and betook [13] himself to the Chersonese, and there fortified three forts.—*Alcibiades,* 7.

[1] *Diuturnus.*

[2] *Honor.* This word may often be translated by " office."

[3] *Domi militiæque.*   [4] *Trado.*

[5] That, after a verb of asking, *ut ;* that not, *ne.*

[6] " Nor was that," etc.

[7] Cf. *Rem ex sententia gerere* and *rem minus ex sententia gerere.*

[8] *Invidia.* May also be translated envy or unpopularity.

[9] *Ex quo fiebat ut.*

[10] Cf. *tribuere aliquid culpæ.*   [11] *Tyrannis.*

[12] *Abrogare magistratum alicui.*   [13] *Se conferre ad.*

XCVII. *SALLUST.*

Their birth, age, and eloquence were, therefore, almost equal; their magnanimity[1] was the same, also their fame; but[2] the one had different qualities from the other. Cæsar was considered great through[3] his kindness and liberality,[4] Cato through the uprightness[5] of his life. The former[6] became renowned for his kindness and pity; severity had added dignity to the latter. Cæsar by[7] giving, aiding, pardoning, Cato by giving nothing acquired[8] fame. In the one was a refuge for the wretched, in the other a destruction for the bad. The good-nature[9] of the former, the consistency of the latter, were commended. Lastly, Cæsar had made[10] up his mind to work, to watch, to refuse nothing that was worthy of a gift; he desired for himself a great command, an army, a new war, where his merits[11] might be conspicuous.[12]—*Catiline*, 55.

[1] *Magnitudo animi* or *magnus animus.*

[2] *Sed alia alii.*   [3] Abl. of cause.

[4] *Munificentia.*   [5] *Integritas* (*in* and *tango*).

[6] *Ille* (that one before mentioned) and *hic* (this one here) may be used for former and latter.

[7] Use gerunds.   [8] *Adipiscor.*

[9] *Facilitas.* Cf. *facilis* and *difficilis.*

[10] *In animum inducere.*   [11] *Virtus.*   [12] *Enitesco.*

H

XCVIII. *CICERO.*

We must[1] undoubtedly die, and whether[2] on this very day or not is uncertain. How then will he who fears death hanging over him every[3] hour be able to main-tain[4] his equanimity? I do not think that there is need[5] of a very long discussion about this when I call to mind that not only Brutus, who was killed in freeing[6] his country; not only the two Decii, who spurred[7] their horses to voluntary death; not only Regulus, who set out for punishment to keep his word plighted to the foe; not only the two Scipios, who wished to block[8] up the road for the Carthaginians even[9] with their bodies; not only your grandfather Paulus, who by his death atoned for the rashness of his colleague; but that our legions often set out with cheerful[10] and buoyant spirits to that place from whence they never thought they would return.—*De Senectute,* 74.

---

[1] " Must " may often be translated by part of the verb.
[2] Mind this depends on " it is uncertain."
[3] Abl. of time when.   [4] *Animo consistere.*
[5] *Opus est* with abl.   [6] Use the gerundive.
[7] *Incito.*   [8] *Obstruo.*   [9] *Vel.*
[10] *Alacer et erectus animus.*

XCIX. *CÆSAR.*

Having beached[1] the ships and strongly fortified the
camp, he left the same[2] forces as[2] before to[3] guard the
ships. He himself sets out for[4] the same place from
whence he had returned. On his arrival there already
greater forces of the Britons had assembled from all
sides to that place, the chief[5] command and conduct of
the war having been entrusted by common design to
Cassivelaunus, whose[6] territory is separated from the
maritime states by a river which is called the Thames,
about eighty miles from the sea. The Britons alarmed
at our arrival had put[7] him in command of the whole
war and government.—*Bell. Gall.* v. 11.

[1] *Subduco.* To launch is *deduco.*
[2] Same—as, *idem—qui.*
[3] Use *dativus propositi* of *præsidium.*
[4] *Eodem.*
[5] *Summa imperii.*
[6] Turn this passive sentence into Latin by an active one.
[7] *Præficio,* with accusative of person (put in command) and dative
of what he is put in command of. *Præsum* with dative means " to
be in command of."

C. *NEPOS.*

Conon the Athenian began[1] his public career in the Peloponnesian war, and in it his aid was[2] of great service. For as prætor he commanded[3] the land forces, and as captain of the fleet he performed great exploits by sea. For these reasons especial honour was paid[4] him. For he alone was in command of all the islands. While in this office[5] he took Pheræ, a colony of the Lacedæmonians. He was also prætor at the end of the Peloponnesian war, when the forces of the Athenians were beaten by Lysander. But at that time he[6] was away, and on that account the affair was worse managed. For he was both skilled[7] in military matters and a careful commander. Consequently, at that time it was doubtful to no one that if he had been present the Athenians would not have[8] sustained that defeat.—*Conon,* i.

[1] *Accedere ad rempublicam.*
[2] *Magni esse.* Cf. *tanti esse, parvi pendere, non flocci facere,* etc.
[3] *Præsum* with dative. *Præficio* means to put in command of.
[4] *Habeo.*   [5] *Potestas.*
[6] *Absum,* to be away ; *adsum,* to be present.
[7] *Prudens rei militaris* or *rei militaris peritus.*
[8] When the verb is in the pluperfect subj. in the direct, it goes into the future participle with *fuisse* in the oblique narration. Thus—

    Si milites tentassent urbem cepissent.
    Dixit " milites si tentassent urbem capturos fuisse."

CI. *CICERO.*

But before I come to that which is the proper[1] (business) of your inquiry, I think I[2] should refute[3] those things which have been asserted often in the Senate by his enemies,[4] and in the assembly by unprincipled[5] people, and a short time since by his accusers; in order that, by[6] every mistake being removed, you may be able to see clearly the matter which is coming for[7] your decision. They say that it is not right for that man to live who admits that he has been guilty[8] of homicide. In what city, pray,[9] do most foolish men argue thus? In that forsooth which saw the first capital[10] trial of the gallant[11] Horatius, who when the state was not yet free was acquitted by the assembly[12] of the Roman people, though he admitted that he had slain his sister with his own hand.—*Pro Milone,* 3.

[1] *Proprius* followed by genitive.
[2] Put this passively by using gerundive.
[3] *Refuto* may be used. As a rule don't use the Latin word from which the English one is derived, e.g. *familia, obtinere, officium* cannot be translated by family, obtain, office.
[4] *Inimicus. Hostis* means a public enemy.
[5] *Improbus.*   [6] Abl. abs.
[7] *In judicium.*
[8] Lit. "that a man has been killed by him."
[9] *Tandem.* Often used in this sense.
[10] *Judicium de capite.*
[11] The Latins put another substantive in apposition; so *Horatius, vir fortissimus.*
[12] *Comitia. Comitium* is the place of meeting.

CII. *SALLUST.*

When this was reported to Cicero, alarmed by the double [1] danger, because he was no longer able to protect the city from treachery [2] by his private judgment, nor was he [3] clear how [4] great the army of Manlius was or with what design (it had assembled), he lays [5] the matter before the Senate. Consequently, as is usual in a case of danger, the Senate passed [6] a decree that the consuls should use [7] their best endeavours to prevent the state from suffering [8] any harm. That is the greatest authority which is delegated [9] by the Senate to a Roman magistrate, viz. to raise an army, to wage war, to restrain in every way the allies and citizens, to have the greatest military [10] and judicial power at home [11] and abroad. On other occasions, without the order of the people, a consul has no authority [12] over any of these things.—*Catiline,* 29.

---

[1] *Anceps.* (*An-caput,* lit. two-headed.)
[2] *Insidiæ.* Sometimes it means ambush. Cf. *struere insidias.*
[3] *Satis compertum habere.*
[4] Dependent, of course.　　　　　[5] *Referre ad.*
[6] *Decerno ut,* or omit the *ut.*
[7] *Dare operam ut* or *ne.*
[8] *Aliquid detrimenti capere.*　　　　[9] *Permitto.*
[10] *Imperium atque judicium.*
[11] *Domi militiæque.*　　　　[12] *Jus.*

CIII. *CÆSAR.*

Put the speeches into Oblique narration.

The leaders and chiefs of the Nervii who had any ground [1] of friendship with Cicero say that they wish to confer [2] with him. When an opportunity was granted them they say as follows: " All Gaul is up in arms; the Germans have crossed the Rhine; the winter quarters of Cæsar and the others are being attacked; you are mistaken if you hope for any assistance from those who distrust [3] their own cause; we, however, are so [4] well disposed towards you and the Roman people that we refuse nothing but winter quarters; you may [5] depart in safety [6] from winter quarters through our country, and set out without fear in whatever direction you please." Cicero replied to this: " It is not the custom of the Roman people to accept any [7] terms from an armed foe."—*Bell. Gall.* v. 41.

[1] *Causa.*   [2] *Colloquor.*

[3] *Diffido* with dative.

[4] *Hoc animo*, abl. of quality. Cf. *Bono animo sum erga te*, I am well disposed towards you.

[5] When *may* means "it is allowed," use *licet* with dative.

[6] *Incolumis.*

[7] Translate "any" in a negative sentence by *quisquam* or *ullus;* in a positive sentence, when all are included, by *quivis* or *quilibet.*

CIV. *LIVY.*

Then having summoned the people to a meeting,[1] "That which," said he, " you have often desired, O Campanians, viz. that you should have the power of inflicting[2] punishment on a wicked and abominable[3] Senate, such power you now have, not by tumultuously[4] storming the houses of individuals, which they defend with garrisons of dependents[5] and slaves, with very great danger to yourselves, but in safety and freedom. Yet[6] do nothing hurriedly[7] or rashly; for I will give you the power of passing sentence on each man's life,[8] so that each one may pay[9] the penalty that he has deserved.[10] But above everything it behoves you so to[11] gratify your anger as to think that your safety and interests are superior[12] to your anger. For, as I imagine, you hate these senators, but you do not wish to have no Senate at all, since you must[13] either have a king, which is an abomination, or a Senate, which is the only council of a free state."—xxiii. 3.

[1] *Contio.* This is a contraction from *conventio.*

[2] *Sumere supplicium ex aliquo* or *afficere aliquem pœna.*

[3] *Detestabilis.*   [4] *Per tumultum.*

[5] *Cliens.* Derived from Greek κλύω, to hear.

[6] The Latins would say, "Nor do anything." Use *quisquam* because the sentence is negative.

[7] *Raptim.*

[8] *Caput.* The Latins also use *caput* when we should say souls.

[9] *Dare pœnas* or *pendere pœnas.*

[10] *Emereor.* Look out the meaning of *stipendium mereri.*

[11] *Indulgere.*   [12] *Potior.* Use abl. of comparison.

[13] You must, etc., may often be translated by the gerundive. So here use *habendus.*

CV. *SALLUST.*

Relying[1] on such friends and allies, at the same time because there was a great amount of debt[2] throughout all lands, and because most of Sulla's soldiers, having squandered[3] their property, mindful of plunder and their old victories, were desirous of civil war, Catiline formed[4] the plan of crushing[5] the state.   In Italy there was no army;[6] Cneius Pompey was waging wars in distant lands; he had great hopes if he were a candidate[7] for the consulship; the Senate, indeed, was in no wise on[8] its guard; all things were safe and peaceful; but this was very suitable for Catiline.   Therefore about the[9] first of June in the consulship of Cæsar and Figulus, he first of all (began) to[10] speak to individuals; to exhort some, to try others; to show them his resources, the unprepared condition of the state, and the great prizes of the conspiracy.—*Catiline,* 16.

[1] *Confisus* with dat. or *fretus* with abl.

[2] *Æs alienum,* lit. money belonging to another.   Cf. *sum in ære meo,* I am solvent.

[3] *Largius uti.*

[4] *Capere consilium* or *inire consilium.*

[5] *Opprimo.*   Use the gerundive, and observe, though construed actively, it is really passive.

[6] *Exercitus (exerceo,* to drill) is the general word ; *acies,* an army in battle array ; *agmen (agimen)* when on the march.

[7] *Petere consulatum.*   [8] *Intentus.*

[9] Lit. about the kalends of June.   When were the Greek kalends ?

[10] Use historical infinitives.

CVI. *CÆSAR.*

When[1] now the fight[2] had been going on for more
than six hours, and not only strength, but also missiles
were failing our men, and the enemy were pressing on
more fiercely, and were beginning to cut down the
rampart and fill up the ditch, and matters were now come
to[3] the last extremity, Publius Sextius Baculus, the[4] chief
centurion, whom we mentioned as being disabled[5] with
several wounds in the war with the Nervii, and also
Volusenus, a tribune of the soldiers, a man of great tact
and valour, run up to Galba and inform him that there
was one hope of safety, if by[6] making a sortie[7] they
should try a last resort. Consequently, having summoned
the centurions, he quickly informs the soldiers to[8] cease
fighting for a short time, and to refresh themselves from
toil; afterwards, on a signal being given, to[8] make[9] a
sortie from the camp and to place all hope of safety in
valour.[10]—*Bell. Gall.* iii. 5.

[1] *Quum* with the slightest idea of cause in it is followed by subj.
[2] Use *pugno* impersonally.
[3] *Ad extremum casum.*
[4] *Primopilus* or *primi pili centurio.*
[5] *Confectus.*　　　　　　[6] Abl. abs.　　　　　　[7] *Eruptio.*
[8] What he actually told them was "cease fighting, etc." The
imperative in oratio directa goes into present or imperfect subj. in
oratio obliqua. Use here therefore the 3rd person plural of imperfect subj. of *intermitto.*
[9] *Erumpo.*　　　　　　[10] *Virtus*, most literal transl. "manliness."

CVII. *CICERO.*

You see what the question[1] is; now consider what must[2] be done. In the first place I think I must[2] speak of the nature of the war; next of its magnitude, and then about choosing[3] a commander. The nature of the war is of such a kind that it ought especially to arouse and inflame your minds; in it is[4] at stake the glory of the Roman people, which has been bequeathed[5] to you by your ancestors, not[6] only illustrious in all affairs, but unrivalled in military matters. At stake, too, is the safety of your allies and friends, in[7] defence of which your ancestors waged many and dangerous wars; at stake, too, are the surest and most valuable revenues[8] of the Roman people, in[9] the event of which being lost, you will lack[10] both the embellishments[11] of peace and the sinews[12] of war; at stake, too, are the fortunes of many citizens whose interests[13] you ought to consult both for their own sake and that of the state.—*Pro Lege Manilia,* 2.

[1] *Causa.*

[2] "Must" may be often translated by the gerundive. Cf. *Hoc mihi faciendum est.*

[3] Use the gerundive, and recollect, though translated actively, it is really passive. Cf. *Homines proni sunt ad amandam voluptatem* (for pleasure to be loved).

[4] *Agi* is to be at stake. [5] *Trado.*

[6] Not only, etc., may often be translated by *quum—tum.*

[7] *Pro quâ.* [8] *Vectigal* (*veho*), properly a duty on things *carried.*

[9] Lit. "which being lost." [10] *Requiro.*

[11] *Ornamenta.* [12] *Subsidia.*

[13] *Consulo tibi* means I look after your interests; *consulo te,* I ask your advice.